THE
UNDERTOW
OF
HEALING

THE UNDERTOW OF HEALING

KATIA MIYAMOTO

atmosphere press

For Dalal, Jamie, Ayla, and Katie

–

In loving memory of Lieselotte Blaschke

PROLOGUE

AVERY

As the rain patters against my window, I think of how I will die. Maybe I'll be swept away in a storm like this one, maybe I'll be caught in a plane crash or car accident. Drowning seems too cliché when you live in Destin, Florida, surrounded by beaches and waterparks. Hopefully, I'll go peacefully in my sleep when I'm a good age, like 90, but Callista would say that's boring. That's Callista for you, I guess, and she wouldn't take anything less than something dramatic enough to make the headlines. I imagine her skydiving and jumping out of a plane only to find the parachute hasn't been attached or performing a jump on a double black diamond slope and tumbling down the snowy mountain. But for some reason, when it actually happens, I imagine us to be together. Although we've only been best friends for four years, it feels like we've known each other forever. We have an understanding of each other that everybody longs to have at some point with somebody. Together, we are Callista and Avery. We are untouchable.

The thoughts about death and other dark topics are how most of my nights alone go. I've found that they help with my art and what I'm able to create the next day. When you are an artist, you see the world through a different lens. Anything and everything serves a purpose in your art, what you create.

The wind from outside shrieks and rattles my bedroom door, and I give my best attempt to shift my thoughts to counting sheep. Although I don't need to get up early tomorrow, I need my rest to study for finals which are coming up next week. I wonder what Callista is doing at this hour. I know she's not sleeping and definitely not studying, but she would never waste a storm like this. I wouldn't be surprised if she was wandering around in her backyard, documenting the lightning and thunder.

When the winds are still raging, and I'm still awake a half hour later, I give up and switch my bedside lamp on. The hand-painted alarm clock on my nightstand glows green in the light and reads 1:04 AM. As the rain and thunder fall into a consistent rhythm, taunting my restlessness, I scourge my brain for a new art piece idea. It needs to be life-changing, monumental. It needs to be enough to get me into a top art college, enough to make my mother take my career as an artist seriously. It will be.

So far, I'm thinking of—*tap!* Something other than rain hits my window and shatters my built-up thoughts. Knowing it's probably the palm tree in the apartment's front yard, I shove my pillow over both of my ears to block out the myriad of sounds erupting from outside. My effort is futile, and the tapping only grows louder. Giving up and finally slipping out from under my layered blankets, I shiver as I walk barefoot across the cold marble floor of the apartment bedroom. I hate the stupid rain. In Florida, it storms frequently, but it has been suspiciously calm for the past few weeks. I guess this is why. My cold hands fumble with the shutter's cord, and I finally pull it up, only to see a shadowy figure standing in the bushes outside.

My first instinct is to jump back and grab something to defend myself with, and my heart starts to beat wildly in my chest as I try to imagine who could be waiting for me outside my window. I think hard about what I have on the desk behind me. A handcrafted vase I painted in preschool, a chemistry textbook, a pencil holder—thunder rumbles once again, and I startle momentarily, turning back to face the window. I don't see much other than a dark shadow, but lightning quickly follows the rumbles in the sky. The quick flash of light is enough to imprint the image of Callista in my mind. Her blonde hair is tangled and rain-soaked, green eyes dripping in black mascara, water flowing off of her red coat—but she still looks gorgeous in that effortless way of hers.

My fearful expression transforms into one of annoyance as I look at Callista in exasperation.

"What are you doing?" I mouth from inside, blinking in disbelief.

She stares at me like I'm crazy and taps the window again. I make sure she sees me roll my eyes as I go to pull up the window lever. As imagined, she wastes no time climbing in through the opened window. A blast of rainwater and salty air follows her in, and we fight against the roaring wind to close the window again. My best friend drops to the floor dramatically and heaves for breath, leaving puddles of muddy rainwater on the just-cleaned floor.

"What are you doing here?" I hiss, knowing damn well if my mom hears her in my room, she'll ground me for life. My close family hates Callista, but I can understand why. Callista is reckless, spontaneous, and stupid at times like these, but she's fun. I admire her for all of these traits: Callista is everything I'm not. I watch her as she dumps a backpack full of clothes and other supplies on the floor.

"I couldn't sleep," she casually admits, shooting me a wry smile. I know that smile, and I know my best friend.

"Whatever you're thinking, don't," I whisper firmly.

Callista rolls over onto her stomach and tosses me a raincoat. She grins with that gleaming twinkle in her eye, and my shoulders slump.

"Absolutely not."

But Callista is Callista, and she recognizes the look on my face. "C'moonn, please, Aves."

Aves is the nickname she came up with in our first month of friendship; it was the first time anybody ever called me anything besides my boring old name, Avery. She also knows it's my weakness. Callista gives me her best impression of puppy eyes, and I unwillingly smile.

"No."

She wrinkles her nose at me and buttons up her coat, despite the knowing glares I throw her. She never stops smiling, showing off her perfect row of straight white teeth.

"Are you coming, or are you not?" She shoots me a glance as she slides my window open.

She knows I'll follow her, but I don't want to give her the satisfaction right away. Callista knows me better than anybody does—her adventures give me life, and that feeling she leaves behind hits me in the gut every time. I slide my feet into my new boots and throw on the matching spare raincoat she brought me.

"Where are we going?" I ask, converting back to my natural voice once I'm outside in the storm.

She doesn't answer, but winks at me as she skips through the puddles on the boardwalk.

"You're so slow," she playfully shouts over the still-rumbling sky.

The wind nicks at my exposed cheeks, and the rain drills into my skin as if the world is scolding me for following her into the stormy night. I run to catch up with her, my white boots dirtying with every step through the sloshing water.

Callista smiles at me over her shoulder and takes my hand, pulling me forward. My hood falls off in the rush, and the rain immediately soaks my hair, but I don't bother trying to put it back on. I can't be saved.

"Seriously, where are we going?" I yell over the rain, and the only response I get is another all-knowing smile.

Of course, this is another one of her crazy surprises. I wouldn't be surprised if she was taking me out to the middle of the ocean. When we reach her destination and she finally lets go of my shaking hand, pruny from the rain, I realize where she's led me. We are on the docks where the ships are tied so they don't float away in the night, standing in front of her father's yacht. Usually bright white and reflecting the light of sunny Florida, this boat looks anything but inviting. Callista poses in front of the yacht, dangling a pair of gold keys connected to a fisherman's hook keychain. I can hear the tinkle of the keys even through the howling wind.

When I said I wouldn't be surprised if she was planning on taking me out to the middle of the ocean, I didn't think she would actually do it. But now that her plan lies clear in front of me, I take that back. Lightning crackles over the dark sea, lighting up the giant stormy waves that are usually calm, clear waters. She's had many plans before —sneaking into school after curfew, shoplifting from a kid's clothing shop, flashing fake I.D.s to the guy at the old movie rentals place so he would let us rent rated-R movies, but this is the worst one yet. This is where she goes too far.

Callista once again knows me too well and wraps a dripping arm around me.

"It's just for fun. We'll take it out for a bit and put it right back. Nothing's going to happen to us."

I shake my head in disbelief. "What's the point of this? If you want to do something we can just go back to my apartment and watch a movie—something *fun* like that."

Callista turns to look me in the eye and starts to work her magic. "Avery, I promise nothing's going to happen. I've done this before—all the time. I just thought it would be cool to take you out for once because I know for a fact you've never been out during a storm. But if you really want to go back to your apartment, we can."

Reckless Callista has changed to understanding Callista, and her green eyes crinkle at the corners as she smiles at me. I think about saying no again, taking the keys from her, and walking away, but I know no matter what I say or attempt, there's no choice. As if she would ever back down so easily.

"Fine. Just for a few minutes, then we go back."

Her grin widens, and she jumps up and down in a puddle, splashing me. As I shake my head at her squealing and help her untie the ship's rope, I think to myself. Callista is right. Nothing is going to happen to us because nothing happens to happy people who live in the sunniest place in Florida. Nothing happens to best friends since middle school. Nothing happens when you're living in the bubble we live in. I step onto the boat.

As Callista starts the engine and we rev off to deeper on the shore, the boat swings back and forth violently, causing my stomach to turn. Surprisingly, I like the feeling, just like I crave the adrenaline rush I get when Callista and I do something even a little bit against the rules. The mesmerizing high Callista has provided me since 6th grade. I'm still deep in my thoughts when the yacht capsizes, completely flipping over and forcing me down into the cold, raging waters.

I fight a useless battle against the ocean, screaming and crying and kicking to stay up. Every time I open my mouth to shriek for help, the salty water pours in, burning the top of my mouth and my throat. I can't see, I can't hear over the roar of the waves and the pattering of the rain as it hits me repeatedly and the wind icing my skin and—where is Callista? Through stinging eyes, I try to see through the water as I kick toward what I assume to be the shore, but I see nobody and nothing other than the swirling and foaming of the sea. Water fills my lungs to the point where I can't cough and splutter it out anymore, and I uselessly sink down, down, down into the cold water. I'll never graduate. I'll never prove my mother wrong. My art career will never take off. I'll never fall in love. I'll never grow old with my best friend. This is how I'll die.

When I wake up, I'm in what I assume to be an infirmary. Nobody is in the room besides me, and an empty armchair sits in the corner of the room. A place where my mother should be. The white and pastel blue of the walls contrast blindingly with my last sight of the dark ocean. My last sight, my last smell, my last taste of the salty, poisonous water trying to push me down deeper and deeper until I couldn't set myself free. But I am here, and I am alive, and maybe the bubble does exist if I'm still here today, and I will still get to prove my mother wrong and set off my art career and fall in love and graduate and grow old with my best friend. *Callista.* Breathing heavily, I try my best to get up, but my stomach clenches as I push my way up the wire bedframe. An alarm connected to the cot starts beeping, and a red-headed nurse rushes in to sedate me. When I fight her off long enough to ask where Callista is, her face is grim.

CHAPTER ONE

AVERY

One Year Later

School is the last place I want to be right now, two weeks into my summer break. Signing me up for summer school was my mom's genius idea, a plan to get me out of the house and also on track to a top college—two birds with one stone. I've given up on trying to make her see art from my point of view—to her, art is just a cute, meaningless hobby of mine, but career-wise a path to failure, while to me, art is everything I live for. A pit of dread is drilled into my chest as I enter the winding hallway of Henderson High School. Hell on earth. I feel like Henderson High could be a great place once again, with its ginormous courtyard and perfectly air-conditioned classrooms, but for that to happen, the entire student body would need to disappear.

Junior year has been a disaster for me, and what I once considered my escape from home and favorite place to be is now my second prison. As I enter the rising-senior phase, I have no escape from anything anymore. At home, there's my eager mom, ready to pounce and hint to me about the hardships of an art career the second I step through the door, and at school, there are the non-filtered rich kids who have no worries in the world. The non-filtered rich kids I used to be friends with when Callista was around. They now know me as a figment of their past, the tragic story of the girl who once had everything only to lose it all within a year. If you ask me,

I can't tell you which is worse.

I check my paper schedule that's printed on a piece of scratch paper and scan the sheet for my first class. Advanced Placement Calculus is first on the list, to no surprise. According to my mom, math equals logic. She thinks the stronger my mathematical skills are, the less art-infused my thoughts will be. We both laughed when she first told me this, hers triumphant and mine incredulous.

I take in everything around me for the first time in a real two-week summer break as I prepare to enter a lecture full of doodling and daydreams. Chipped lockers and food wrappers on the ground, a cheer tryouts poster on the school event bulletin board, and a half-finished banner I assume to be a welcoming sign for the incoming freshmen. I pause as I pass by a locker that stands out from the dark gray of the others. This is Callista's locker, which I and a few others decorated last year. What once was a tiny yellow door full of photos, messages, and stickers, is now a brown, chipped locker stripped of all decoration.

A janitor wearing a cap looks up momentarily from his job of scrubbing off the remaining paint and glitter from the metal. The pictures of Callista taped to the front of the tiny door and the messages written to her are all gone now, and judging by the trash can next to his feet, I can only imagine where they are. I swallow, and I can hear my dry throat in the back of my head, but I fight to keep my head up and walk past him.

When I turn back for a second, I see the pictures I so carefully placed on Callista's old locker in the tiny trash bin, surrounded by rotting banana peels and torn-up worksheets. A sad kind of rage floods through my mind as I bite my tongue and stare. It's saddening to think that such an important memory can just be tossed in the trash like it's nothing. The photo was the first I had ever taken with the Polaroid I saved up to buy when I turned thirteen. It was one of my favorites of Callista and me, grinning happily on a hammock in Hawaii the summer of eighth grade. The bell suddenly vibrates from the speakers above me in the hall, and I snap out of my trance. I hadn't realized how late it was, and without another thought, I swiftly reach into the trash can and grab the photo, now covered in banana goop. The janitor looks at me like I'm psycho, but I smile tightly at him and run through the empty hall to get to my class.

When I fling open the door and unapologetically walk to an empty desk in the back, the teacher glances at me with annoyance, but I don't care. I let his voice drone on in the back of my head as I start to fill my thoughts with everything but math. The photo of Callista and me seems to tease me as the classroom lights reflect off the tiny Polaroid frame. As heartless as it seems, I try to not think about Callista as much as I can. I know everybody says it's best to forget the bad parts and only think about the shared smiles and secret laughs, but I can't. Every memory related to her always fades into the dark and thrashing sea.

I study that face I haven't seen in more than a year and try to soak up everything about her one more time. Her smile, the dimples I had always been a little jealous of, the ways her eyes would crinkle at the corners when she laughed. I think of how they looked when she was about to cry—the emerald green would fill up with large tears, glossing them over and dripping down her eyelashes. I feel the water pouring into my head, and I pull back my hair as I try to adjust my thoughts.

College, art school. The main piece of my art portfolio I will have to submit by September, in three months, and I have nothing so far. I've been trying to do anything art related for months, but I can't; everything ends up a mess of clay or a crumpled-up sheet of watercolor paper at the bottom of my trash bin. It's not that I've lost my love for art; it's just that I have no motivation, nothing to work with. I'm more than aware that I need to complete my art portfolio, and more than anything, I want to start on my main piece, but my mind swirls and ends up blank each time I try to think about it.

All that comes is a feeling that fills my stomach in a rage of pounding and fluttering and sickens me to the gut. How could I have forgotten? Piece by piece, no matter how hard I try to deny it, *she* is slipping away in my mind, washing away with the junk of my family drama and college and school filling my brain in her place. I grab the picture off the desk and hold it tightly with white hands. I clutch it so hard my knuckles turn red, and sweat from my palms fogs the silky lens of the photo. I don't want to let go. I can't let go.

Lunch comes surprisingly fast, and I am grateful but dreading the rush of students who will pour out of the building and fill up the courtroom with their whispers and judging glances. A year later, and nobody has moved on, least of all me. As chattering and laughter echo around the building, I make my way to a table hidden at the edge of the courtroom behind a large oak tree. This is the spot Callista and I would sit at and eat every day in the ninth and tenth grade. It was just us, Callista and Avery, and everybody knew better than to sit with us. It's not that we were judgemental or cold; it's that there was no better place to be left out than in between us. We had no room for others, although the round, glossy bench seemed to have space for at least five people. Today is no different, and as I throw my tote bag onto the table, I lay my arm against the cold concrete. I am in no mood to eat and just want to go to sleep.

I am interrupted by a gaggle of familiar girls who trot over to the table and place their lunch trays down beside me. By the way they are not acknowledging me and sharing secret glances with each other, I know their gesture isn't one of invitation. A girl wearing a white headband and hand-painted pants I would usually compliment elbows me as she sets her red tray down. I want to say something, something sharp enough to let them know that this isn't their spot and they can't be here, that I was here first, anything to make them leave me alone and not fill up the space that's already taken. My chest betrays me as it closes up and turns my vision to spots. I do not have the strength of Avery and Callista; I am defeated.

I swipe my tote bag off the table and start to stand up when I feel a warm hand grip my upper arm. I freeze, not used to the physical touch, and turn slowly to face whoever it is while the girls' chatter dies. I meet sweepingly dark brown eyes, the same color as mine. They stare at me, and by the way the boy is raising his eyebrows, I understand he's trying to tell me something. I shakily sit down, my tote bag slipping down my hand and hitting the side of the bench with a quiet thud. Mystery guy breaks out into a smile and slides down next to me, shoving in between me and a redheaded girl. He seems to be unaware of what he walked into as the other girls look at each other slowly and then get up to leave.

They walk away whispering little nothings to each other, and I hear occasional phrases of annoyance such as *Who does he think he is?* I don't disagree with them, and I grimace at him, feeling extremely uncomfortable and awkward.

"I'm Avery," I say, trying to sound nonchalant.

"I know," he replies.

He smiles with one part of his face, and his eyes crinkle at the sides just like Callista's did. I swallow.

"You do?" I say, trying to look somewhere other than his face, which I have been staring at since he's gotten here.

"We've had class together; we've just never talked. I'm River."

I feel stupid and embarrassed, and everything from my neck to my forehead flushes a bright red as I nod repeatedly.

"Oh my god, I'm so sorry. I'm just having a rough day; I usually would have remembered."

He laughs. "It's okay. Being forgotten isn't always a bad thing."

I ponder what he says for a minute and try to relax my shoulders. When did it get so hard to talk to people?

"You were friends with Callista, right?" He says this like it's more of a statement than a question, and my shoulders tense up once again out of reflex. It's a sudden and unexpected change of topic, and I'm sick of having questions asked about my role in her death.

"Yeah, I was," I say, my tone naturally getting defensive.

He seems to falter at my newfound coldness, but doesn't stop pursuing the topic.

"I can only imagine how you feel. I know it's been a year, but"—he makes a show of looking around the courtyard—"it never gets easier."

For some reason, I laugh. My wall of defense has temporarily been deactivated for the first time in a while, and I like the feeling.

Somebody is actually talking to me besides Akemi, head of

the school newspaper and desperate for insight into Callista's incident, and insensitive yet curious classmates. River is looking at me in a way I can't quite decipher, and I realize that I've only really known this boy for short of five minutes.

"Why did you do that?" I ask.

He looks as if he's going to ask what I mean but changes his mind last minute.

"It's hard to see people taking advantage of someone—especially one that's been through as much as you."

His words hit me like a rock, and the moment has died. I should have known better than to think that someone would actually see me as just another person rather than a charity case or a reason to be sorry. To my surprise, I'm disappointed. When the bell rings, I grab my bag and slip quietly off the bench, leaving him behind as if I was never there.

For the rest of the short summer day, I can't stop thinking about River. I don't know why, but I'm grateful in a sad way to have somebody occupying my mind besides my mother and dead best friend. Today has been a flop, as expected, and I gather my thoughts in a scramble to pull something out of my brain, something good enough to tell my mom. I learned something new, I scored good on the worksheet I completed in class today, and I made friends. All of these are lies, and I am more aware of it than ever as I pull open the glossy apartment door of apartment 107.

As expected, my mom immediately comes rushing out of the ornately decorated living room to ask me about my day. Her dark brown hair is silky as ever, skin tan and smooth. When people see me out with her, they often assume she is my sister. It's kind of embarrassing to think that my mom pulls more guys my age than me.

"How was your day?" she asks, lips pulled up in a hopeful smile. I know what she wants to hear, but I can't force any made-up detail to come out of my mouth. Instead, I force a smile back at her and nod.

"It was good."

"Good? Not great?" She raises her eyebrows as if I have some untold secret I've been keeping from her.

"My day was wonderful," I say sarcastically, hanging my tote on the wall rack next to the door.

She sighs and pats my shoulder, slightly disappointed, and wanders back to the living room. I hear the TV blast an advertisement for Sprite as she turns the volume up. The first place I go to is my room, my safe place.

Unfortunately, the lilac walls of my room don't protect me from my thoughts, and I am stuck in the constant whirlwind that is my mind. It is hard for me to escape my imagination and the crashing waves and raging wind that come with it, but usually, I am able to block them out after a hot shower.

Unfortunately, the shower doesn't work this time, and as I carve my name into the fog on the mirror with my blue-painted pinky finger, everything comes crashing back into my head. So, I do the next best thing. I flop onto my bed, letting my head hit the mattress, and wait for the tears to fall. As expected, they don't, and the most I can get out of myself is an itchy eye. I haven't cried since Callista's death, and I don't know why.

Usually, people would go to therapy for these sorts of occasions, but like everyone who probably needs therapy, I am convinced I don't need it. I know my mom is worried about me and my newfound loss of friends, outings, and Friday night talks with her about all the exciting things that have happened in my week, but everything has changed. I lean forward and stare quietly into the circular mirror hanging on my wall.

I see a brunette girl with dark rings under her eyes who is wrapped in a light pink cardigan. On good days, I would look longer and try to find what I like about myself. I like the freckles that dot my nose and cheeks, how my bottom eyelashes are longer than the top, and the birthmark above my eyebrow. These things about me make me feel like I'm someone more than what has happened to me. These things make me see myself from somebody else's point of view, just a little naïve high school girl who maybe needs a cup of coffee or a few extra hours of sleep. Someone who has no idea who I am or how I've changed. In a flash of a moment that comes every so often, I hate myself.

Who am I to be standing in front of the mirror feeling like this? "People have it worse than you," a tiny voice repeats over and over in the back of my head. "She would have moved on. It should have been you and not her," it adds. My throat closes, and spots dot my vision. I snatch up the keys that are beneath my pillow and slip on a pair of striped flip-flops. "Mom?" I cautiously say as I gently shut my bedroom door. The only response is the droning of the news lady, and I catch my mom snoring quietly on the couch. Although the living room clock only reads 4:02 PM, I know how much she wears herself out. I wrap a white woven throw blanket around her, switching the TV off.

Today, I have plans. Plans to go anywhere and everywhere I feel like, to treat myself to anything I want. Sure, at times, I feel like I don't deserve to live, but if I'm the one who made it out, I'm going to make the most of it. For me. For her.

CHAPTER TWO

RIVER

I've always been told I'm more of a listener than I am a talker. When people walk by me in the halls, they stare or move aside. Not because I'm intimidating or a sight to see, but rather because I am quiet. Quiet people are not trusted. Quiet people know things. We are observant, quick to think on our feet, nimble, and able to slip by unknown.

However, as satisfying as it might seem to hold some type of unnoticeable power over people, being perceived as mysterious is also lonely at times. My closest friend, Andres, is nothing like me. He is captain of the school swim team, and being an athlete in high school automatically gives him a pass to town-wide popularity. I have a share of his social life in a way; I am respected because people know we are close. This is the only thing that keeps me from being tossed around as the stickler, loner, quiet kid who thinks he is too good for anybody. But somehow, it doesn't feel right. I don't fit in with his swim-team friends or the girls he hangs around. Honestly, I don't really want to.

Having a loving family at home, a full business plan set out for me once I graduate from high school, and a guaranteed spot at one of the top universities in the nation does not grant me the right to be self-pitying. My long days agree with me, and I fill my life with taking care of my little brother Josh, studying business, and reading the long, drawling books my dad provides me with. Although I don't need to score high grades in order to get into the school, I am planning to go to due to the connections my dad has with the board, I find it impossible to not spend at least an hour or two studying or doing homework.

I've had many opportunities to push myself into the spotlight. Being best friends with an athlete gets you a lot of questions as well as attention, especially when you are the polar opposite of him. Apparently, having a lean body and some inkling of intelligence makes you popular with many of the girls, and my dad has been suggesting I get a girlfriend soon to take with me to college. He worries about me, and we all know that a lonely, quiet boy will not be a good image for his company. He plans for me to get married young and have kids probably, something to make me seem more fit to be on the board of a company that designs computer software. I don't complain; I never do. I know I'm lucky enough to have a future designed for me and a firm plan to set me off in life.

"River?" comes my mother's tinkling voice from down the stairs.

I don't feel like answering, but I know if I stay quiet, she'll come check on me.

"Yes?" I call back as loud as I can, careful that she hears me. I wait for a response.

"The weather is nice today; why don't you step outside for a bit?"

I know that her suggestion is actually a demand to get outside and get social, so I roll out of bed. I love my mom, but she worries about me too much, all the time. Because I'm hard to read and prefer to not share myself with others, I'm the family curiosity. I hear her late-night talks with my dad, speaking in hushed voices downstairs, thinking I won't hear.

What if he's depressed?

Do you think we've been too hard on him?

Don't you think something's wrong?

Her constant suggestions to step outside or hang out with Andres are part of it, and I know I'll have no escape this summer. I enter the living room as brightly as I can and smile at my mom, who is sprawled out on the couch, fanning herself with a paper fan. She is pleased to see me with keys in my hand and gives me an overly cheerful smile and wave as I trudge to the front door.

When it shuts behind me, I feel like I've been kicked out—which I technically have. I enjoy going out; usually, it gives me an opportunity to be the River I would like to be all the time. Talkative, funny, easygoing, everything I feel like I can't be at school or at home. But today, for some reason, I feel drained. I can't stop thinking about what happened today at summer school. Although it was a quick encounter, I can't help but feel like it is the most interesting thing that has happened to me all year. There is something about Avery Hill; I just can't quite put my finger on it yet.

My dad is at work, and my younger brother is with him, probably helping him with coffee and napkins and enjoying the appraisal he receives. I could visit them ... but do I want a lecture on what comes after college and a tour of what will be my office when I graduate? Not really.

Thinking of the places there are to go in our small town and finally deciding on the boardwalk, where Andres is working at an ice cream shop this break, I trudge through the sandy path outside of my house that will lead me to the beach. I usually love being in nature alone, but summer is not the time for me. The hot sun burns through my black T-shirt, and I curse myself for not changing into a thinner layer in this weather.

Kids play on the shore, a few miles away from me, but I can still hear their squeals and screams as they run away from the water. I'm thankful when I finally arrive at the boardwalk and stop to catch my breath at a shaded table.

The boardwalk is as crowded as ever, and I can see why. During summer, this is the perfect attraction for teen girls and tourists, with its mini roller coasters, large neon lights, and the sweet smell of cotton candy wafting through the air. I almost smile as I look around for The Cheery Cherry, the ice cream shop Andres has scored a summer job at. I'm not surprised that it's the bright red-and-yellow building with dancing cherries painted on it so large that I can spot it from the other end of the park.

As I make my way to it, my eyes are somehow drawn to a girl sitting alone on a bench next to the Ferris wheel. The neon lights flash above her and light up her pale skin to red, green, purple—she glances up and finds me immediately. I startle but try to play it off, a strange reflex of mine, considering I'm not used to feeling flustered and being caught off guard. We briefly make eye contact, and I quickly realize that it's the same girl from summer school today. Avery Hill, Callista Kobb's best friend before she passed. I want to say something to her, but she gets up from the bench and stands in line for the Ferris Wheel, so I turn around and hurry to The Cheery Cherry. Andres looks up in alarm when he hears the ice cream bell sound, but he heaves a sigh of relief once he sees it's me. I stifle a laugh when I look at him dressed up in a red apron and cherry-shaped hat, and he shoots me a look.

"If one more sticky little kid walks in here asking me for a banana split, I'm going to quit."

I snort. "How did you even get hired here?" I ask, scooping chocolate chips from the toppings bowl into my hand.

Andres looks offended. "I'm the perfect salesman for ice cream!" He flexes his muscles, and I grimace.

"You also hate kids and get grossed out by everything, like a prissy baby. I'm surprised you're not wearing a mask and gloves."

He rolls his eyes and offers me a seat behind the counter. I gladly accept and reach for more chocolate chips when a voice startles me.

"You're not supposed to do that." I swing around, and a tall Asian girl in a uniform grins at me.

She laughs when she sees my expression and puts her hands up. "Chill. I was just kidding."

It's Akemi Ito, the head of the Destin High School Newspaper. Known for writing in the corner of the classroom and badgering people for insight into Callista's death the entirety of junior year.

I laugh slightly. "How's the ice cream business? Andres was just filling me in on how great it's going."

The bell sounds suddenly, and we all turn our attention to the door, where Avery Hill walks in. I feel like I'm drowning as a chocolate chip slides down my throat, and I try my hardest not to cough out loud. She seems surprised when she sees me sitting behind the counter, with my eyes watering and cheeks turning red, but thankfully she turns to Akemi.

Akemi looks overjoyed to see her. "Avery! Hi! I haven't seen you in forever."

Andres looks at them awkwardly, conversing as he stands at the cash register. He shifts back and forth, and I realize I've never seen him uncomfortable like this. Avery walks up to the register holding a scoop of mint chip ice cream covered in chocolate chips and chocolate syrup and fishes out her wallet.

Andres is still staring at her in a way I can't quite make out, and Akemi and I turn to look at each other. Taking control, I pull my chair up to the register and reach over the counter to weigh her ice cream.

"Seven dollars and fifteen cents," I read off of the scale.

She pulls out a ten-dollar bill and slides it over the counter. I try to make conversation as I input the information into the cash register.

"That's a lot of chocolate sauce for a scoop of mint chip," I say.

"You can never have too much chocolate," she grins back at me.

This interaction is weirdly light compared to the first time we actually spoke today. She's smiling wide and I can see the freckles spotted across her nose as it scrunches up. When she sees me staring, she quickly drops her smile, almost as if she's embarrassed.

"Keep the change," she says, blowing it off.

She takes a spoon and her ice cream and begins to walk out of the shop, pausing in the doorway. She looks like she's about to turn back and say something, but the door shuts, and the tiny bell attached to the wall tinkles after her. It is weird in the ice cream shop, and Andres is still unmoving behind the register.

"Andres? You good?" Akemi breaks the silence.

He tries to play it off, but I know him better. "Wasn't she Callista's friend?"

Akemi seems overjoyed by the question and a chance to bring up Callista Kobb, but I know why he asked now. She nods, and I look at him, giving him a questioning stare as he pretends not to notice.

He shrugs. "I just thought she looked familiar, that's all."

24

Andres is saved from further questioning momentarily as the shop's bell sounds suddenly.

A group of kids clutching wads of cash in their tiny hands enters the shop chattering, and I get up from my chair. "I should probably get going."

Akemi looks disappointed that the conversation is over so quickly, while Andres seems like a weight has been lifted off his chest.

"That sounds good. Come visit us tomorrow?" he says quickly as the kids start to line up.

I nod and wave as Akemi writes something down on a mini notepad. No doubt it's about Andres' weird behavior towards Avery Hill. Even though it's been months, she, for some reason, won't quit the idea of a story on Callista's death.

CHAPTER THREE

ANDRES

When Callista Kobb died, I knew within me that it was my fault. I never meant for anything bad to happen, but I doubt anybody would believe me if I told them. Callista was spontaneous, bright, and bubbly—everything you would imagine a high school girl in Destin, Florida, to be. But she was different, and she knew it. That was her superpower. While other girls would flock to me during swim season, she stayed away. Callista was smart enough to know that, over time, I would come to her. I did. We were a perfect match, so it seemed. We were so scared to let anything destroy it, so we kept it to ourselves. I can see how it might have been selfish now, but it was nice having something to myself for once. One thing we had in common was how adventurous we both were. Finding someone like that, someone who understood my want to get away in the middle of the night, my sudden changes in plans, seemed like the biggest blessing there could be. Little did I know it was a curse. A curse that would cast a dark shadow on us all, the entire town of Destin. All because of me.

The night of the storm, we had been playing this long-term game we had created. Every week, we gave each other one dare to complete. If completed, we both gained one point. Whoever had the most points by the end of our junior year would have to buy the other a Yamasaki Jet Ski—the newest model and something everybody in Destin would die to have.

I will never forget the bask of the phone's glow on my face that 2 AM. The messages we had sent back and forth chiming over the sound of the pounding rain on my roof.

She would do anything with me. I'm going to get this point

That prissy girl? Good luck, Cal, but I think you owe me a Yamasaki ;)

You'll see after tonight

And I did see. I saw on the news the next morning, a flood of Instagram stories, a notice on the school board.

The whistle blows, and I push all thoughts of Callista out of my mind as I focus on the pool in front of me. Jackson, the newest member on the team, is competing in his 200-meter freestyle race, and as expected, he is far in the lead of all the other schools. Nobody is surprised, but we all cheer and clap for him like a sports team does. There are a few shouts and whistles that come from the bleachers, but we all are hoping deep inside that he will mess up. Everybody here is working towards the same thing as me, and it's a well-known fact that less than half of us will make it. A scholarship at the University of Florida for swimming is the dream that pushes us to hold our breaths longer, to kick a little harder, to not give it a rest until every joint in our body is aching.

I move up a chair when Jackson and the other teams' swimmers exit the pool as the overhead speaker announces Henderson High School as the winner of this round. When the coach ushers me forward to the diving stand, I don't feel anything. The rush I used to get from swimming, the pounding of my heart when

I was called up to the stand, the butterflies in my stomach that would swim around to the rhythm of the water, the adrenaline pumping through my arms as they fought—it's all gone. It's been gone for a while, but I haven't and won't ever let it show. My dad would never forgive me. I would never forgive me.

The countdown starts, and then the whistle sounds, and I dive smoothly into the water, cutting the clear surface crisp as I kick my way to the top. Lifting my arms over my head, I don't need to glance behind me to know I'll be the winner of this round. But when I pull up to the edge of the pool, panting hard and pulling off goggles, I am not met by cheers or high fives from my teammates.

The team coach stares at me from the bleachers in disbelief, and I don't realize why until the overhead speaker announces Roanne High as the winner of this round. My round. As soon as I'm out of the pool, I toss my swim cap on the ground. All of my teammates get up from the bleachers to meet me, but I don't want to talk to anybody right now. I grab my swim duffel bag and slip out of the pool gates before they catch me. I don't know why I'm not as bothered as I would be last year if I had lost a round. If I had lost even once a few months ago, I would have run straight to the gym and practiced my arm and leg exercises I've been training with since I was in elementary. I would have practiced late into the night until my muscles were sore. But right now, I don't feel the drive, motivation, anything. I don't know how I feel.

I wonder what my dad would have said had he been able to make it to my round. He's not the sympathetic type, so I expect I'd be met with a series of curses and a shaking head.

I'm busy taking the lock off of my bike outside the pool

when my coach jogs up to me. I can only imagine what scolding he has prepared, and I brace myself for the shouting that will fill my eardrums in a second. But when he reaches me, it's much worse.

"I expected better from you," he says, and I'm left speechless.

Normally, anybody else on the team would apologize for poor performance, but I'm not sorry. Today I've decided to be tired. I'm tired of trying to fit myself into the mold of a perfect athlete, son, and student. Swim captain, straight As, an asshole with friends to flock to him, and a party to go to every other day. Coach is staring at me in the way people do when they expect something from you. He wants me to say I'm sorry. He wants me to promise I'll train all day and night until I reach my full potential. He wants the best from me, but I can't help but wonder if that is the best *for* me.

"Andres." The voice is sharp, firm, demanding.

I can fix this in a second with two words. I can continue on the path that I'm on to a swimming scholarship at a top university, my classmates' approval, a—

I fish my swimming cap out from my duffel bag and throw it on the pavement in front of him. "I quit the team."

I'm just as stunned as he is at the moment, and without another word, I shove my bike lock deep into my duffel bag and mount my bike. He says something as I pedal away, but I can't quite make it out.

"You'll be back" or "You don't mean that" are both strong possibilities, but I don't need to think about that right now. I focus on the iciness of the wind on my wet hair and the cars that slowly surpass my bike. Nothing can stop me—except for the street light blinking green.

As soon as my pedaling stops and I lean a foot on the

ground to keep my bike steady, the thoughts swarm my mind.

What have you done? You're nothing without swimming. Your entire future down the drain, gone. Take it back while you can. Email Coach and tell him you were delusional. No. *Wow, that's a cool car. I wonder what model it is.* Better. *You're a murderer and a quitter.*

I look up sharply, as if everyone around me can hear my thoughts as well. Cars are paused, waiting to turn the corner, but nobody is looking at me. I tousle my wet hair and observe as I try to quiet the thoughts raging in my mind.

A familiar car catches my eye. A silver Volvo with tinted windows is paused in front of me, and a family of three sits inside. Although I can't hear into the car, I can see mouths moving furiously and a shaking hand pointing from the steering wheel. Family fights. I'm almost jealous as I watch the three of them talk. The girl in the passenger seat turns suddenly to face the window, and I almost jump back in shock. It's Akemi, her long black hair covering half of her face. She looks furious, breathing hard into the window, and it's not until the light turns green and the car rolls away that she sees me. We make eye contact for a second, an invisible string in the air reaching into her car and connecting her to me.

I wonder what she's thinking at the moment. I wonder if we'll talk at The Cheery Cherry and we won't remember this. I wonder what the fight was about. When the light signals me that it's okay to cross the street, I walk my bike across the road and let the confusion wash over me like a cool tide.

Later that night, when I lay awake in my bed once more, staring at the ceiling, I don't think about my future and what my dad will do when he finds out. I don't think about college and scholarships and the upcoming Friday night bonfire. I don't think about Coach and what the rest of my team thinks of me right now. I don't even think about Callista Kobb, and the guilt that once consumed me every night is nowhere to be found. No, the tiny thought that dances into my head tonight is Akemi Ito.

CHAPTER FOUR

AKEMI

The day Callista Kobb died was the worst day of my life. Not for obvious reasons you might think, such as her death, but rather something a bit more selfish. I was dumped for the first time. For most people, being dumped sucks but they have the sense to know that they'll be alright again in time.

For my dramatic self, it was the end of my life. His name was Bryce Levine, which is probably one of the most basic names in the world. But to me, he was anything but basic. I loved the way his eyes seemed to change color from green to blue depending on the lighting, his hyena-like laugh, even the way he would slather his hair in gel every day before school. I guess you could say I notice the little things about people, but honestly, the thing I liked best about him was the fact that he was my first boyfriend.

It wasn't that guys weren't into me; it was the realization that they would never be able to handle my double lifestyle. Growing up in a household with strict immigrant parents isn't exactly the same as having chill, nonchalant Floridian parents who let their kids go to beach bonfires every night without a curfew. Bryce was the first person who I felt really understood me and the way I lived when nobody else would even take the time to really get to know me. So, when he broke up with me by text right when I had woken up, it shattered me in ways I had never thought possible. The worst part of it was the way he left.

I don't think this is working out, Akemi. Hope we can still be friends :)

For a writer, that was probably the most insulting way a guy could have broken up with me. I had romanticized the idea of romance since I was just a little girl, dreaming of what love I would experience in the future. Never in a million years did I think I'd be heartbroken over a text ending with a smiley face from a greasy high school dude. For most writers, a rage like this would fuel their work. A collection of sad poetry, a series of angry letters, or a novel based on a protagonist who had gotten their heart broken by someone who didn't deserve them. Strangely, it did the opposite for me. I felt as if my obsession with writing and late nights ignoring calls to work on articles for the school newspaper had actually ended my first and only relationship. I also felt jealousy. Jealousy had always been a prevalent part of my life, especially when I had been surrounded by tan, model-perfect girls since I was born. Girls who wouldn't have been or let themselves be dumped like this.

When I thought of someone who I would gladly trade lives with, I immediately thought of Callista Kobb. That girl had everything. Fun parents, a perfect face and body, a loyal best friend, and boys tripping over her feet. Writing skills and high SAT scores don't matter when you have everything else in life. People like that just seem to glide through anything without any setbacks. So, when I heard of Callista's accident, all of my values were shattered. It shook me to the core. I had never thought that something as tragic as the death of the town's it-girl would strike such a sunny place like Destin.

I had never even considered that something as tragic as the accident would happen to someone as perfect as Callista. But life moves on, no matter what happens and no matter how much we're begging for a break. And that's exactly what happened over the past year. Everyone moved on silently, rebuilding the school's social hierarchy and rebuilding the haunted city's reputation. I think the person it hit hardest was Avery Hill.

Avery and I had known each other since preschool but only started talking near the end of elementary school when I got her to sign my petition to introduce creative writing as a class. It never happened, but at least I had almost made a friend. She started to come over almost every afternoon to do homework, and my parents were beyond happy that I'd finally made an actual friend. When she met Callista, everything changed. She stopped coming over and instead went shopping at the mall with the new cool girl in town. I was aware from a young age that people like Callista always got whatever they wanted, and I had tried to be her friend for years, hoping that maybe I would be able to have a share of her happiness.

Although when the accident hit, Avery and I hadn't talked in months besides our occasional small talk in the halls, she was the first call I made. She understandably hadn't picked up, but I realized I was too invested in swallowing my tears about Bryce to be much of a good comfort anyways.

I'm glad to say that a lot has changed since a year ago, and I'm much happier on my own. I managed to snatch a job at The Cheery Cherry, the ultimate ice cream place of Destin, which bought me time to myself during the summer to figure out what I wanted to do next. I knew getting a job, no matter how small, was the first step to living the life I had always dreamed of. A life filled with excitement and fun and love and the freedom to live the way I wanted. My passion for writing, however, had not come back to me. I had fallen into a year-long slump, and my articles for the newspaper were half-assed. The only story worth getting was an insight into

Callista's death, which I had already halfheartedly attempted to research for the entire year.

I'm on my way to The Cheery Cherry for my after-closing clean-up shift, and my mom has so graciously offered to give me a ride to the boardwalk. I know it's because I'm rarely at home anymore and she doesn't have enough time with me to pressure me to talk to our relatives in Japan or take on a summer course to learn Japanese and be able to connect with our family more. And deep down, I know it's selfish, but growing up here, the only thing I've wanted is to fit in. I want to grill hot dogs on the Fourth of July down at the beach in a new bikini or go surfing with some guy I just met on the boardwalk.

"Akemi," my mother says, her accent thick. "How is your work going?"

"It's going great," I say as casually as I can, turning away from her to look out of the window.

My dad hums in the backseat of the car.

"You are never at home anymore." She speaks in a steady tone that I know is disappointed in me.

"I don't have time."

She breathes out a huff of air that I know is her way of saying *Yes, you do.*

"We only have family in this lifetime. You should spend more time with us."

I'm angry because that's what I've been told my whole life, but we had never done anything to make us seem like a "family" to me.

Birthdays, Christmas, and Halloween, all normally family holidays, weren't celebrated at all. Time spent together with the three of us was rare, and most of my conversations with my parents had to do with other relatives and disapproval of things I had wanted to do. All of the little stupid things to them that meant the world to me for *some* selfish reason.

I focus on my breath fogging up the window as the car rolls to a halt at the red light. I can hear my mother in the background, but it sounds like she's miles away. A form of ignorance I've perfected after years of practice. A familiar face catches my eye on the sidewalk. Andres. My coworker and a huge deal at school, being swim captain and head of all of the airheaded jocks. Our eyes meet momentarily, and I'm caught by surprise at how he looks. His disheveled hair is dripping water onto his blue shirt, no doubt the result of a swim meet. He looks the same as he always does, but something feels different somehow. I can't quite put my finger on it, but I wonder if it has to do with Avery Hill. I think about yesterday, the awkward tension between them at The Cheery Cherry. Something she hadn't seemed to notice, but the way he more than noticed it made it obvious that something was up.

My mom's voice snaps me out of my trance-like state, and I sigh. If only I had an outlet like I once did, something to rely on. Writing had been my escape for so long, but now I'm just not quite sure how to ease back into it. When I wrote, I was happier. I was free, I was independent, I was able to express myself and actually have a voice that mattered. My articles would be spread across the school to people who didn't even know who I was. But they would read, they would observe, and they would agree or disagree. They would see me. And as the thoughts start to flood my mind for the first time in forever, one clear light stands in the way. Andres McQueen and Avery Hill and Callista Kobb.

Whatever is going on, that story is mine.

CHAPTER FIVE

AVERY

For the first time, I feel excited when I arrive at school. I haven't felt this way since at least a year ago, and I like the sensation that rolls around in my stomach like the comfort of a hot tea. I wonder if I'll see River today at lunch. I hope I'll see River today at lunch. But even the newfound excitement that has wrapped around my mind is not enough to protect me from the whispers of the scattered student body. *Chin up, Avery.* My pace quickens until I finally reach my locker at the end of the hall, and I grab my textbook from inside. I keep my locker open for longer than necessary, taking the time to finally breathe and hide my face from the gaggle of girls in the corner. I wonder what it would feel like to be normal now. The new normal. The bell rings, forcing me to surrender my locker-door shield, and I try not to look like I'm rushing as I rush to the classroom.

The lecture seems longer than usual today, almost as if time is dragging its feet in retaliation to my desperate need for lunchtime. But when the bell does finally sound, a surge of anxiety sweeps through me. All of the things I haven't taken the time to consider ambush my thoughts, and I remember the group of girls, the strange looks, and the way River had defended me as if I couldn't fend for myself. Which, even though I couldn't, still made me feel ashamed and almost spiteful. As I make my way to the large oak tree, I spy a familiar head of brown hair. A smile stretches across my face before I can stop it.

"Hey, what's up?" I muster up as casually as I can. It feels like the first time I've talked to someone in ages. I don't know why I'm so nervous.

"The sky," he answers as if he's known me for years and years on end, and I groan. All pent-up anxiety has now evaporated because of his dumb joke, and I'm thankful.

"Very original."

He shrugs, and I carefully sit down on the bench beside him. It's nice to have a friend, or even just an acquaintance. Just somebody to sit next to, really. Someone who doesn't make me seem like I'm so delicate I can't be talked to normally, or a walking *Dateline* case. We sit in silence for a while, my thoughts screaming at me to say something as he unwraps a burrito.

He points to a rolled-up canvas in my bag and looks up at me. "Is that a painting?"

I grimace. "It will be, soon."

He gives me a puzzled look, and I explain further. "I haven't been able to actually paint, since—you know ..." I trail off.

He nods in understanding. "I get it. I'm sure you'll be back to it in no time. I remember seeing your artwork on the cover of the yearbook freshman year. You won the schoolwide contest, right?"

I laugh, letting the memories flood over me like warm water. "Never been prouder. If only a sketch of Destin's class of 2019 on the beach would get me into an art school."

He seems impressed. "You want to go to an art school?"

I nod. "My portfolio is due in September. I have yet to make my final piece."

He raises his eyebrows and gestures to my bag. "Planning on doing it at school?"

"Honestly, I'm aiming to finish it by the end of the summer. Next period I have advanced art theory, so hopefully, class will whip me into shape on time." I'm only half joking, and I really am dependent on that class to get the spark started in me again.

"That makes sense, because if anything's going to get you painting again, it's definitely the yelling of Mrs. Stewart." He laughs. "I can't believe you're taking art in the summer."

"My mom wanted me to take calculus, and I told her the only way I would do summer school is if in the afternoon I took an art class as well. Guess it worked." I shrug.

He nods slowly, raising his eyebrows. "Nice ultimatum."

When school ends, I feel as if I've learned something more than just the definition of a derivative. I've learned that it's nice to talk to people again. It's nice to sit in the same spot as I did with Callista a year ago, even if it's with another person. It's nice to laugh and talk normally and introduce myself to someone who didn't quite know me before.

I'm making one last stop at my locker to drop off my textbooks when I see someone waiting for me. It's River, to my surprise, and ignoring the looks from people in the halls, I walk up to him.

"Hey. I was wondering if you were free this weekend?" He looks at me, and I blink.

This weekend is the weekend of June seventeenth, the anniversary of Callista's death, and I've been planning on staying home.

"This weekend really isn't the best time for me ..." I don't know what to say without bringing everything up and making it awkward between us, but he understands.

"I get it, June seventeen and all. That's actually kind of why I was wondering. A few people wanted to have a bonfire down at the beach in remembrance? It's not really anything official, but I think you might like it if you came."

I'm taken aback because it had never occurred to me that people would have made plans on that day. "Sure," slips out of my mouth before I can hold it in.

He smiles. A real, genuine smile. "I'll see you down at the boardwalk then, Saturday at seven PM. We can walk down to the beach together."

This afternoon, when I get back from school, I finally have something to tell my mom. She's waiting by the door like she always does when she knows I'm coming back home, and for once, I'm excited to see the look on her face.

"How was your day at school?" she asks, a hopeful look lighting up her youthful face once again.

"Great," I smile.

CHAPTER SIX

RIVER

It's times like these that I think about my future. Laying alone in bed, staring at my ceiling, tired from the day. I wonder how tired I'll be in a year from now. I wonder if, in four years, I'll be that successful company manager that my father dreams of me being. I can't live in the present no matter how hard I try; my mind will always take me to the past or future. My phone screen lights up, and the time reads 7:36.

I roll out of bed and prepare to head downstairs, where dinner is bound to be set on the table. My brother, Josh, runs down the stairs two steps at a time when he hears me open the door. I smile and shake my head, jogging after him.

"No running in the house," my mother declares from the head of the table when we come into view. She smiles at me, and I know she recognizes that there has been a change within me the past few weeks.

Ever since summer school began, I have been able to focus on my studies and fulfill my father's hunger for some sort of progress report. I've also been lighter in general. Avery Hill, no matter the short time I've known her, has made me feel more like myself than I have in a long time.

Josh mashes his potatoes up with a fork, and my father stares at him in disapproval. "That's disgusting, Josh. Eat your potatoes normally."

"I like mashed potatoes better!" He pouts at my father,

and I wink at him.

"Use a spoon; it works better."

My father meets my eyes with a heartfelt sigh, and I fight the urge to laugh.

"River's in a good mood, huh?" my mother raises her eyebrows at me.

Josh claps his hands. "He's probably in loooove."

I raise my eyebrows at him. "I'm not in love, but thanks for that thought, Josh."

My father looks up at me from his plate. "Nobody special?"

I resist the urge to roll my eyes. The carefree feeling I felt a moment ago is slowly diminishing. I can feel the energy at the table change.

"I would have thought you'd find someone by now. It's the end of high school, after all." He nudges my ribcage, and I grimace.

My mother can sense the shift in my mood and chimes in. "It's just that I think you honestly could use the influence of a nice girl in your life right now, River."

I resist the urge to laugh. That is the most ridiculous reasoning she's come up with, by far. My parents fell in love in high school and have been together ever since, my father the successful owner of a computer software company and my mother a high school counselor. They are a strange pair when you think about it, but they have similar views when it comes to parenting me.

My father is worried about my future in terms of taking over his company successfully, while my mother is worried about my social and mental well-being. They both agree that a relationship would benefit me greatly, my father's reasoning being a good look for the future of his company and some proof that I wasn't a social pariah, and my mother's being I was alone all the time and it worried her. She had once even told me that she was doubtful I'd ever get married at all. I had spat out my water at that dinner table talk.

My father sets down his fork.

"Son, I know we've been hard on you these past few years, but it's only because we worry about you."

I don't know where this conversation is going, but I can't remember the last time my father had actually set down his fork at the dining table in the middle of a medium-rare steak.

"I also know that your heart might not be entirely where we want it to be—and that's okay."

I swallow dryly in disbelief. My mother takes his hand in hers, and it's clear they've had this conversation before.

"I admit, I've been putting a lot of pressure on you about the future of the company and shaping your image. But we don't have to worry about that right now. What we do worry about"—he gestures to my mother—"is you."

Josh jumps up from the table, breaking the awkward streak.

"Bye!" he shouts as he runs up the stairs.

Nobody else moves.

I feel like I need to say something now, with both of my parents looking at me in a way I can't quite figure out. Before I can get anything out, my mother looks at me with tears in her eyes.

"We just want to know that you're okay, River. You're alone all the time now. Andres never comes around anymore. It would make us really happy to see you getting out more. You work so hard ..." she trails off shakily.

I give my parents a knowing look. "I have to work hard. What about the company? It's almost my senior year, and I'm almost at the finish line. I'm okay."

My father sighs. "Don't worry about the company right now."

I blink up at him. *What?*

He almost seems to be enjoying my state of confusion as he takes a slow sip of water.

"I can tell that your heart's not in it. I actually don't think it's ever been. We'll figure all that out later."

I feel like I'm dreaming, and I shake my head a few times to wake myself up. "You knew all this time?"

I don't get any response.

My mother chimes in again. "We just want to see you happy."

I am speechless, for once, and the silence in our dining room is overwhelming.

"Does that mean I get the company now?" Josh shouts from the top of the stairs. He has given away his hiding spot, and it's obvious he's been eavesdropping this entire time.

My father picks up his fork and spears another slice of steak. "You were probably expecting something different, huh?"

I don't say anything.

"You make your own choices, son. You've always been free to. You just never did."

CHAPTER SEVEN

ANDRES

It's nearly midnight when I decide to wake River up. He's sleeping, no doubt, because he isn't like me. He goes to bed in a timely manner every night—if you call him past ten, you won't get an answer. I am considerate enough to not wake up the rest of his family, although his mom would probably be overjoyed to see me. I consider her close to a second mom—she's known me since I was in kindergarten, after all. I wonder what her reaction to me quitting the swim team would be.

I pick a pebble off of the sidewalk and chuck it at his window. It hits the middle with a loud *thwang*. I wait, instead of picking up another one, because I know River is a light sleeper. On the camping trip in seventh grade, River had woken up at every possible sound, convinced it was a bear or mountain lion or something with claws big enough to rip him into pieces. Sure enough, the curtain shifts, and I see River's groggy face looking down at me. I gesture towards the front door, and he disappears. The door creaks open a second later, and River stands in his red plaid pajamas.

"Andres?" he asks incredulously.

"Can I come in?" I say, already pushing my way through the door.

He sleepily closes the door behind me, not bothering to answer. I'm the one who leads him upstairs to his room, and he trails slowly behind.

"Why are you here so late?" he asks.

It's only 11:57, which isn't late in my book. It's actually pretty early to me and the rest of the guys I know from school. I sigh. Here goes.

"I quit the swim team."

The sleepiness is gone from River's eyes in an instant, and his jaw drops. "You're kidding, right?"

I shake my head, and he knows better than to question me. It's rare that I'm serious like this, and it's obvious that something is off. River jumps off his bed and stands over me, hands in his hair. I want to laugh and tell him he looks ridiculous, but he genuinely seems distraught.

"Why would you quit?"

I shrug, and he raises his eyebrows exaggeratedly. "I just wasn't feeling it anymore."

His jaw unhinges once again, and he sits back down on the bed. "Andres, you're not going to 'feel it' all the time. That's normal. It's not normal to quit something you *love*, especially after all these years."

"I didn't come here so you could talk me out of it. I just wanted to let you know." I'm firm, and he knows it's hard to sway me.

He doesn't know what to say. "Did something happen?"

I take a deep breath. "No."

I falter. "Everything's just ... I don't know."

River knows me too well, and although I'm a good liar, he can sniff out the truth like a hound dog. I'm used to lying—small little white lies to my parents, such as where I am on Saturday nights, why my grades are slipping, why I would be home late. Over the past year, I've gotten better. It's hard to say if I really had gotten better at lying or just shutting people out. Not telling your classmates and friends about the girl you had once loved and then killed kind of confuses you.

What he says next is enough to shock me out of my shell for a second. "Does it have something to do with Avery Hill?"

"What?" I immediately counter, mind racing with thoughts. *Does he know? How would he know?*

"I saw the way you looked at her at The Cheery Cherry the other day. I've never seen you like that before, and I've known you for my whole life."

I try to play it off by laughing, but it comes out as a nervous sound that tickles the back of my throat. "How did I look?"

He's serious as he leans back in his bed. "Scared."

I am speechless. "Scared? Me? Of who—Avery Hill?"

He shrugs, observing me. "I wouldn't know. Do you have a reason to be scared of her?"

This night could not get any worse. I shake my head in disbelief. "No, I don't have a reason to be scared of her. But you seem to have taken notice of her, haven't you?"

He shrugs again. "I guess I have."

I swallow. "Well, I would be careful if I were you."

River furrows his eyebrows and props his head up on a pillow. "What do you mean?"

The words come tumbling out of me faster than I can process them. "Haven't you heard? She killed Callista Kobb." My face is red and flushed, and my stomach is twisting wildly. I feel like I'm going to throw up, and I do—word vomit. "Middle of the ocean, same boat, early morning, and only one of them made it out alive? Think about it."

River stares at me for so long that, at one point, I think he can see through me. His jaw clenches, and his eyes harden. "You're a dick."

This is the first time in my life I've ever heard River say something even remotely vile. When we were younger, he was the only one of the guys to never succumb to saying the curse words we weren't allowed to say until we were a certain age. He had something about respect, and we all knew it. He respected the people on the streets of Florida, the substitute teachers that everyone would torture with spitballs and dumb questions, everyone in his life. But looking at him now, there is something different in him. And in his eyes, the dark brown eyes I have known so well since I was a little kid, I see no respect for me.

I can feel the blood rise furiously to my cheeks as I stutter. "Whatever, man. I'll see you at the bonfire."

When I shut the door behind me, I resist the urge to fall to the floor on his doorstep. Everything is spinning, and the damp air of Destin is thickening in my lungs with every inhale. It thickens and thickens until I can't breathe, until I'm clawing at my throat and gasping for air, until, at last, I can finally feel the merciful cold push of air from out of my lungs.

This is how she felt.

But she never got the chance to take another breath.

CHAPTER EIGHT

AKEMI

I have never been so happy to serve a demanding seven-year-old girl a scoop of sprinkled-covered strawberry ice cream. But today, when the tinkling bell first sounds, I jump at the thought of having someone else in the shop besides Andres and me—even if it is a sticky-handed, pigtailed girl. For the past couple of hours we have been working, there have been maybe just short of ten words spoken.

Andres isn't his usual self today, and my playful nudges that usually get him to joke back at me aren't working. Which is bad when it comes to worker dynamics and even worse when it comes to getting the story about Avery and Andres. I need that story by the end of summer if I want to get back on my writing streak.

Next year, the school newspaper will start off big. It will gain more attention once again and rise in popularity while also motivating my personal writing and future success in school. The perfect win-win situation. The only thing I need to do is get the story straight about Callista's death. What happened before, after, who was involved, how people were feeling. Even a year after, Callista's accident has remained the top story of Destin. But what if I could give the people more?

Andres sighs loudly as he refills the hazelnut ice cream tank.

"Alright, quit the crap."

He startles, my words cutting through the quiet jazz music in the background.

"You've been moping around all day, which might I say is terrible work time etiquette? You work at an ice cream shop, for god's sake."

He cracks a grin for the first time today. *Finally.*

"I apologize if I've been scaring off the kids, but quite honestly, I think I'm doing us both a favor." He winks in typical Andres fashion, and I can see that he's almost back to himself.

"Seriously, what's up? Are you okay?" I genuinely do care, and I look at him as he falters.

"I just didn't get much sleep last night," he admits. "I quit the swim team."

I suck in a deep breath. *Wow.* Out of reflex, a caption flashes in my mind. *Swim captain quits after three years.* I blink the thought away quickly and scold myself.

"You quit? Why?"

He breathes out a laugh, sliding the lid back on the ice cream carton. "I'm getting tired of answering that question."

I don't press further and laugh back. If I want to ask him about Avery later, I need him to trust me.

"I'm just surprised, that's all. I didn't see that coming."

"Neither did I."

By the middle of the day, when it hits prime ice cream time and the shop starts to fill with swimsuit-clad middle schoolers, Andres and I are back to our normal bantery rhythm.

But it's nearly the end of our shift when he asks me what I've been waiting for the entire time. "Hey, are you busy tonight?"

I smile knowingly behind the counter where he can't see me. "It would depend," I say slowly. "Have anything in mind?"

"Well, there's actually a bonfire tonight out on the beach. It's the anniversary of ... you know ... and a few of us thought it would be nice to do something in remembrance of her."

I grin. "Definitely a tribute, not an excuse for underage drinking and fireworks."

Andres seems uncomfortable, and I worry that I've come off too strong.

"I'll be there," I say quickly, trying to cover my tracks.

He tosses his apron at me as he walks out the door. "Seven PM, I'll see you soon."

When I arrive at my house, my mom and dad are sitting on the couch together, watching the news. It's almost a ritual for them to sit down together for at least an hour or two every day of the week and just watch Channel 9. I admire the way they are so in sync with each other, almost as if in a ritualistic dance. Unspoken words and a passed remote, the lowering of the volume, a cushion moved to the other side of the couch.

"How was work today, Akemi?" my dad asks from the right side of the sofa.

I smile. "It was good."

My mom turns around to face me. "Will you be joining us for dinner today?"

A pang of guilt erupts in my chest.

"Actually, there's a bonfire tonight. It's in remembrance of Callista Kobb—remember her?"

At the mention of Callista, my parents look at each other with sadness.

"Of course you can go, *Akemi-chan*. What a horrible thing that happened to that girl."

I grimace and nod. Of course my parents understand when it comes to Callista. Even from beyond the grave, she has a power over everyone. A power that I'm going to delve into in my next piece. A piece that will change Destin, that will re-order the social hierarchy, that will jumpstart my writing career.

Rummaging through the bottom drawer of my dresser, I look for something suitable to wear to a bonfire. The first real party I've been to—ever.

You're not there to party, I remind myself. *You're there to get news. Insight. Research.*

Inner me shrugs. *Same thing.*

I find a white off-the-shoulder top I had bought years ago but never worn. I had seen Callista wearing the same one at the mall, so I walked right into Hollister to find it. I sigh wistfully as I remember when everything seemed to be so shallow. All of my biggest problems were if what I was wearing was cool enough and how much sun-in to put in my hair to make it less black. More like theirs. *Hers.*

When did we all get tossed into the deep end?

I throw on the white top with a pair of shorts and slide my feet into some strappy sandals. As I clip in some pearly hoop earrings and a matching necklace, I don't forget my winning accessory. A light pink notebook and pen.

CHAPTER NINE

AVERY

The sun is setting in Destin, and I can't remember the last time I've seen a sunset like this. The sun sets every day in Florida, and it's always beautiful, of course. But it strikes differently when you actually take the time to appreciate it. I notice how the streaks of orange seem to be melting into the ocean, and the billowy cushions of white are shifting with the warm summer breeze. I feel a flutter in my stomach when I think about how vast the sky seems to be, never-ending and dimming with every second. Or maybe that's the effect he has on me.

I glance over at River as he walks beside me, hands in his pockets. It doesn't take much to shift my attention away from the sunset and to him instead. He is wearing a light green button-down T-shirt, complete with white billowy pants and sneakers. I realize how put together he always seems to be. Self-consciously, I glance down at my paint-splattered crew-neck and shorts.

It's times like these. I wish I had Callista here with me. She wouldn't have ever let me go to a bonfire looking like this. We would have spent at least an hour in her closet, pulling out clothes I would have never worn on my own and trying them on until we found a perfect fit.

As we get closer to the beach, I can smell the smoke piling out of the rock pit in the sand. Chattering grows louder, and a beat is playing from a set of portable speakers. River takes my hand and leads me down the stairs, where a group of at least one hundred people is scattered. I almost expect them to stop the music and everything they're doing and just stare when my feet touch the sand, but to my surprise, nobody takes notice that I'm here.

"Do you want something to drink?" River shouts over the noise, and I nod my head.

Once he's gone, I take a step back. Everything seems so normal now, people laughing and dancing in the sand with cups in their hands. It's been so long since I've actually seen something like this—let alone been a part of it. I'm only now starting to realize how alone I am when River isn't here, when I see someone looking at me from across the party.

It's Andres McQueen, captain of the swim team, and he looks at me with something in his eyes that I can't quite decipher. *Disgust? Resentment? Sorrow?*

I just now realize that Andres is River's friend, and I am surprised when I think about it. It doesn't seem like they have anything in common, but my thoughts fizzle out in an instant. Who am I to judge, anyway? Plenty would say Callista and I were opposites.

Thankfully, my short staring contest with Andres is interrupted by a swooping hug. As black hair tickles my nose momentarily, I recognize the distinct smell of vanilla and pinewood. Akemi steps back and gives me what I can only describe as a Cheshire-cat smile.

"Avery, you made it!" she squeals almost forcefully, and I fake a smile.

"I didn't think I was coming at first, but here I am," I reply.

"Well, I'm so glad you're here now," she says.

Akemi's grin seems to widen almost impossibly, and she

takes my elbow. She wastes no time getting into it.

"So, the anniversary, huh?"

I try to hide my grimace. "It's supposed to be a celebration for her, right?"

Akemi shrugs. "It's definitely a party."

"But speaking of celebrating her, I had something else in mind."

At the moment, I am almost tired of talking about Callista, and I scourge my mind for an excuse to leave. I scan the bodies on the beach for any sign of River with my drink.

Akemi continues. "I want to write a feature on her, just like I was planning on doing last year. But instead of making it just an article, a-a news report, I want it to be big. An interior look."

She spreads her hands as if painting me a picture mid-air, and I nod slowly.

"Wow. That's great. Good luck on that," I say, not really believing her.

The last time she had said she wanted to write something on Callista, she never did. She asked around school for months, but apparently, nothing satisfied her. I don't know why she still hasn't given it up.

Akemi fidgets with the sleeve of her white top. "So, I was thinking ... maybe you could be my first feature." She pauses for dramatic effect, and I lick my lips.

I already know I'm going to say no, but I give her a chance to speak anyways.

"You were her best friend, after all, and there's nobody better than you to talk about—"

She's cut off when River appears at my side holding two cups.

I thank him in my head as I take one of the cups and smile brightly at Akemi.

"Good luck on your article!"

River raises his eyebrows as he leads me down the beach. "Article? Is she still trying to get a story on Callista?"

I nod. "It's been a year, and now she wants to write about it, apparently."

He shakes his head. "That is pretty weird. But then again, when does anything happen in Destin?"

What he said was meant to lighten the mood, but instead, it does the opposite. I agree. When does anything happen in Destin? When it didn't, before, life was good. Life was easy and enjoyable and everything I thought it would always be like, until something did happen. And after that, nothing has been the same. *Nothing will ever be the same.*

I change the subject. "You and Andres are friends, right?"

He seems surprised at the question. "Yeah, we are."

But the way he says it doesn't seem like he means it. I watch as he glances over to the main crowd of people and spots Andres sipping something from a cup.

He looks back at me. "Why?"

I try to play it off by laughing. "I just don't think he … likes me very much."

Something in his expression changes for a second, and I wonder what he's thinking. I wonder if he and Andres have talked about me before. If maybe he knows why Andres seems to be so strange around me. For a second, I think he's about to confess something big, but it must be a trick of the firelight.

"Andres is like that with everyone. It's nothing personal." He sits down in the cool sand, and I sit next to him.

I want to tell him that it's okay and I know that isn't true, because Andres has always been one of the most sociable people in school. Always going out with his buddies, king of the courtyard and the swimming pools. As silence strikes us suddenly, I fear that I've made everything awkward once again. I bite my lip worriedly, wondering if I should say something else.

Callista would know what to do in situations like these, and I try to channel what she would say in my mind. But I can't think of anything, and I wonder what she would say if she even knew I was at a bonfire on the anniversary of her death, sitting under the night sky with a boy. Suddenly, the ghost of a smile flickers over River's face.

"Are you free Monday night?"

This is not what I was expecting, but I am pleasantly surprised. I am also cautious. "Why?"

River has a glint in his eye. "I need you to do me a favor."

I blink at him, putting my now empty cup in the sand. "What type of favor?"

"Come over for dinner."

I'm glad I have finished my drink because I would have choked had I still been sipping on it. He seems amused by the expression that I can't hide and elaborates.

"Just one quick dinner. I want to prove to my parents that I have friends."

My stomach falls a little at that word, but River Aviera has asked me to dinner.

I smile slyly. "What's in it for me?"

"You owe me a favor, remember?" he jokes back.

"A favor?" I genuinely question.

He looks at me pointedly. "I saved you from all those girls back there on the first day of summer school, didn't I?"

I laugh. "So that wasn't just a good deed from the bottom of your heart, then?"

He shakes his head, grinning. "Every good deed comes with a price."

He is so wrong, and I'm about to make fun of him for it when something explodes over me in the night sky. Glittering specks of green, blue, and white rain down on us, and I laugh, realizing it's a firework. Three more erupt, and I watch as the darkness is lit up by sparkles of rainbow, gleaming as brightly as the sun on a hot day. Almost as bright as the smile River flashes me when he takes my hand and runs down the beach.

CHAPTER TEN

RIVER

Tonight, when my family sits around the dinner table once again, it is my turn to surprise them. Our family dynamic has shifted more than I thought possible in the last few days, and I feel shockingly light. Earlier today, I took Josh out to the beach for the first time in what felt like forever. We used to go all the time when I was younger, Andres included. Josh loved to toss a football around, and we all joked that he'd become a star football player one day. The day Andres joined the swim team, Josh magically decided he was too cool for football. Now he wanted to be a swimmer. I wonder why.

Andres has always been the cooler older-brother type. The type Josh would probably love to have as his actual sibling. I am quiet, not as fun as him, and, like I've been told—always buried in a pile of schoolwork. Today at the beach, Josh had asked at least five times where Andres was. In typical little-kid fashion, it was hard for him to take my answer—that he was busy with swim practice. I didn't have the heart to tell him his idol had quit the swim team.

Now sitting next to Josh at the table, it seems like he's forgotten all about today. He picks happily at his oven-roasted Brussels sprouts and is actually eating normally for once. I wait until my mother starts loading her plate with vegetables to tell them my good news.

"Is it okay if I bring someone over for dinner tomorrow night?"

The room is silent as my mother and father stare at me dumbfounded.

Josh bounces up and down in his seat. "Is it Andres? Is he coming over to see me?"

I pause. "It's not Andres, actually. It's someone new."

I swear I can almost physically see my mother's ears perk up. My father looks equally interested.

"A girl?" my mother asks slowly, setting her napkin down on her lap.

I smile. "Yes, she's a girl."

My father pats me on the back and guffaws. "I always thought it was impossible!"

I roll my eyes now. I had thought of this idea quite a while before the bonfire. Knowing how worried my parents are about me makes me feel guilty, like I'm not doing enough. I know for them that showing them one thing will calm their stress. My original plan had been to invite Andres over during the daytime, so my parents could see that I was, in fact, hanging around with people. It felt like they didn't even believe me when I would tell them I was going out, or even to the bonfire on Saturday night. But after what had happened a few nights ago, that has no longer been an option. In all honesty, I'm not complaining.

Avery and I had gotten closer over the past week of summer school and our bonfire experience, and it felt like a breath of fresh air to have someone other than Andres to really talk to. I can sense that she somewhat feels the same, having little to nobody to talk to after the incident. And while it is hard for me to let people in, for some unknown reason, it is safe around Avery Hill to open up. I know my family will love her, as they will love any person I bring home—as long as I don't show up alone, everything's perfect.

My mother is tearing up across the table, and Josh is gagging on a Brussels sprout.

"Are you crying, Mom?" I ask incredulously, and she lets out a shaky laugh.

"I'm so proud of you, honey; you have no idea."

There is a silence that fills the dining room as my father and I make eye contact, and all of a sudden, we're all laughing. Me because it is so relieving to see my parents happy like this, and them because how ridiculous was it to ever worry about me? Josh laughs loudly, too, trying to cover up the way he doesn't understand what's happening between us. Heck, I wouldn't either if I were his age. We laugh our way through the end of dinner, clinking glasses and sharing stories, and for once, I let myself loose around my bizarre little family.

After dinner, I do what I so rarely do and head over to The Cheery Cherry. I haven't talked to Andres since the night he showed up at my house, but I don't like it when we're fighting. Or not even fighting—I don't know what to call the unusual gap of silence that stands between us now. Having settled things with my family in a way that seems impossibly obvious and easy, it seems like the next thing to do is make amends with my best friend.

Even though I'm not the one in the wrong, Andres has a history of never coming forward with anything. Confrontations, apologies, he just stays silent and stays back until everything's fixed. Which, in my case, means I need to fix it.

The boardwalk is not as crowded as usual tonight, which is understandable for a Sunday evening. The familiar smell of cotton candy wafts towards me, and for a second, under the bright lights of the Ferris wheel, I expect to see Avery sitting on the bench once again. Instead, it is occupied by a little girl and her mother, and I smile to myself. I'm seeing her tomorrow. At my house. With my family. *How wrong could that go?*

The Cheery Cherry is almost never busy on nights like these, which is surprising for an ice cream shop in the summertime. I can spot the bright red building from a mile away, and I notice that one letter of the light-up sign has dimmed. As expected, I see no customers through the wide windows of the shop. The lights are on inside, as it's only 8 PM, and Akemi and Andres sit behind the counter. Akemi is swatting him with a cleaning rag, and Andres is laughing hard. Laughing in the way that is so hard your stomach hurts, but you never want it to stop. He looks happy. Happier than I've seen in a long time, since he started the swim team and hanging around with the other jocks every Friday night. Since Callista died and everything changed, and he did too.

I turn around and walk away.

CHAPTER ELEVEN

ANDRES

I can't focus on my job today, which is saying a lot when my job is serving ice cream to kids on the boardwalk. There is so much on my mind—even more than there has been the entirety of the last school year. On top of everything I'm keeping in, I'm also not talking to my best friend. Even if I want to, I can't talk to him. What am I supposed to say—how am I supposed to explain myself?

Yeah, sorry, I completely dissed the girl you like and told you she was a murderer. It's probably because I'm actually the murderer, and it makes me extremely uncomfortable to be in close proximity to her knowing my actions cost her best friend's life and could have cost her life as well.

I wonder how long I can keep this secret. It has only been a year, and it's already turned my life upside down. I'm not swimming anymore, I haven't slept soundly for months, and I've lost more than half of my friends—including my childhood best friend, who is probably the one person on Earth to know me outside of my reputation. I guess this is what you call *karma*.

Akemi sits on a stool behind the counter. She leans her head against the cool tile wall, and I snort. She looks at me.

"I can't believe we're actually waiting for people to come in here," I shake my head.

She sighs loudly.

"I love ice cream, but sitting here for hours on end and staring at these yellow walls makes me dizzy. Is anything even real?"

A tinkling sound comes faintly from outside the shop, and I gesture to the window. "I know why nobody's in here."

She cranes her head to see and gives up. "Why?"

I point. "The ice cream truck is here."

Sure enough, a retro-themed ice cream truck is sitting outside the shop in the boardwalk's parking lot. It has been making its rounds all day, seemingly taunting The Cheery Cherry as it slowly trails by, a gaggle of kids following.

Akemi makes a show of slowly banging her head against the wall. "You're kidding."

Maybe it's the dizziness that comes from smelling ice cream for three hours straight or the mind-shocking effect of the red-and-yellow theme of the shop, but we burst out laughing. We don't stop until the ice cream truck is gone and the chattering of kids outside has faded away.

I hold my stomach. "I think we deserve some ice cream after this."

She checks the cherry-shaped clock on the wall. "Forty minutes till we're done. I say it's a necessity to be able to continue."

I grin and tap the side of my head. "I like your thinking."

Akemi scoops Raspberry Mango Sorbet into a small cup, and I grab a large cone and fill it with Rocky Road. While she makes fun of my enormous appetite, I realize that for the few minutes we've been laughing, I've forgotten all about my problems. Nobody has made me feel this way before, not even River.

In fact, it has always been the opposite with him. River is thoughtful and responsible, therefore always making sure to hold me accountable against my will and never giving me real room to breathe. Akemi is like the first breath you take in after racing across the pool underwater for one minute. Maybe this is what I've needed all along.

We finish our ice cream, constantly flicking scoops at each other, and I spy something falling out of her purse.

"What's that?" I ask, pointing.

I regret it almost immediately because if I've learned anything over the years, it's to never ask what's in a girl's purse.

She quickly snatches it and shoves it back into her bag.

"Just a notebook," she casually shoots me.

"Oh yeah," I say, remembering. "I saw you with that at the bonfire. You were ... writing something?"

She looks taken aback for a moment, but smiles. "Yeah, just taking some notes."

I'm curious. "On what?"

Akemi doesn't look at me as she tosses her empty cup into the trash can. "Just a summer assignment for next year."

"Summer assignment at a party? Wow, I never knew you were so dedicated," I tease.

She looks at the clock. "Five minutes until we should be done. Do you say we should just leave now?"

I'm disappointed because I want to spend more time with her. Although our shift is pretty long, it feels like the only time I'm really alive. I am suddenly desperate as I watch her reach the door.

"Are you free right now?"

CHAPTER TWELVE

AKEMI

I am more than happy when Andres asks me to grab a bite with him after work. Not only because a tiny cup of sorbet is not enough to fill me, but also because it gives me time alone with him outside of a work environment. The perfect opportunity to do some digging on Callista and Avery. We have decided on the Beachside Bistro, only a ten-minute walk from The Cheery Cherry. Although this place is like a home base to most of the kids at Henderson High, I've never been here before. It feels strange to admit. I can see why it's such a big hit among Destin high schoolers, with its seemingly ceaseless supply of pool tables and arcade games. I sit in the window booth of a seagull-themed corner in the diner, and Andres slides in across from me.

This is weird, to say the least. Captain of the swim team—or former captain—and me. Akemi Ito, head of the newspaper, and not really anything else. Not really anything to any of the people who know who Andres is. I realize that I hadn't thought clearly about this before agreeing to go.

Does this classify as a date? Are we hanging out as friends? Why would he even want to hang out with me anyways—what's wrong with his never-ending horde of buddies?

I shake the thoughts out of my head. Of course, this isn't a date. This is strictly a coworker hangout. And also a perfect opportunity for me to get my hands dirty. I glance down at the purse in my lap. I have a good memory, so I'm not too concerned about writing anything down tonight. I'll make sure to journal when I go home, if there's anything to journal about.

Andres orders blueberry pancakes and a Coke, and I get the same. What I'm really craving is the saba misoni from the seafood side of the menu, but for some reason, I'm not comfortable ordering in front of him. When our food comes, a serious look spreads across Andres' face. I look at him in concern.

"Here's our game plan," he says.

I furrow my eyebrows at him.

"We're always talking at work, dilly-dallying—yada yada yada," he says in a mock-serious tone.

I stifle a laugh.

"But I want to get to know you, Akemi. You're my favorite coworker, after all."

I blink at him. "I'm your only coworker."

He points his fork at me and nods.

It takes a second for what he first said to sink in. *He wants to get to know me?* A million thoughts race through my head. For some reason, I can't imagine myself as someone to get to know. It's hard to think that he can see me like that. But I can't let this get in the way of why I'm really here tonight.

Andres is everything a girl here wants. Jock but not dumb, cocky but not too extreme. I do like Andres and my time with him at work, but all of that can come later. What comes first is me this time. Meaning this story and this success.

I look at him, brushing my long hair over my shoulder. "So, what did you have in mind?"

He smiles as he spears a piece of pancake. "What about a speed-question round?"

I raise my eyebrows at him. "A what?"

He elaborates. "We ask and answer questions from each other in a rapid-fire style. Not too deep, whatever first comes to your mind."

I start to think tactically. "Nothing deep? This game sucks."

He starts on his third pancake. "You earn your way to deep."

I lean back. Fair enough.

"I'll start," he says.

"Favorite color?"

"Purple."

"You?"

"Orange."

I'm taken aback by this because there is no possible way anybody's favorite color could be orange, and I burst out laughing. He scoffs at my reaction and waves his hand in the air defensively.

"Not what you're thinking. A sunset orange. Something soft like that." It is my turn to ask a question, and I think of something quick.

"Favorite song?"

" 'Drops of Jupiter,' Train."

" 'This Love,' Taylor Swift."

We move quickly through favorite movies, bands, and subjects. The questions start to get longer and consist of feelings and quick thoughts. It's my turn now.

I take a tentative sip of my Coke as Andres watches.

"First reaction to Callista Kobb's death?"

His jaw slackens, and he clears his throat. "Surprised—I guess?"

I nod understandingly. "Me too."

I want him to be able to open up to me, to trust me with whatever has happened. I know it's deeper than it seems, but seeing the way Avery and Andres interact, it's obvious there's something else. He knows.

Andres is staring at me in almost a blank way, and although it is his turn to ask me a question, he stays silent.

"Guilty," he says so low it's almost a whisper.

"What?"

A beat.

"I felt guilty when I first saw the news," he says clearer.

Something in my heart stops. I don't understand. It was a boating accident. Why would he feel guilty?

After a moment, Andres shakily starts to unravel the story of his relationship with Callista. I feel a sharp pang in my chest when he talks about their understanding of each other, but I can't move a muscle. I am frozen—in time, in disbelief, in denial. He talks about the series of dares and the Yamasaki Jet Ski, the texts, and how it was all to get Avery out into the storm. My stomach twists. Avery clearly doesn't know about this. Nobody does.

When he finishes, he seems to be holding his breath—just like I am holding mine. It is clear that he wants me to say something—anything—and it's all I want to do, too. But I can't.

I place my bag on the table with shaking hands and slowly get up from the booth, careful not to hit my head on the hanging ceiling light.

"Bathroom—really quick," I stutter, internally smacking myself for not playing it cool.

He swallows and nods, and I can feel his stare burning into the back of my linen T-shirt as I head to the ladies' room. Once inside, I let the cool breeze of the air conditioning chill my heated face. I place both hands on the sink and look into the mirror, still shaken.

I have my story, don't I? And it's definitely a hell of a story. Life-changing, monumental, enough to reshape the entire societal hierarchy of Destin. But watching Andres relive his experience and seeing the deep sorrow that crossed his face is almost enough to make me give this up entirely. *Almost.* Or is it? I quickly smooth my hair down, shaking my head a few times to un-rattle myself.

When I arrive back at the booth, something is wrong. Andres is red-faced and stares up at me with an expression of hurt? *Anger? Betrayal?* My jaw drops momentarily at the sight of my open notebook on the table, Andres' name written in bold across one page, Callista's on the other.

"Notes, huh?" he rasps, and before I can stop him, he's gone.

As I defeatedly gather my belongings and ignore the screaming in my head to run after him, I spy something else on the table.

The bill already paid, a purple heart drawn messily in the margins.

CHAPTER THIRTEEN

AVERY

What do you wear when you're about to meet someone's parents? This is probably one of the last things I expected to worry about this year, but as I look at the pile of clothes on my closet floor, I feel helpless. I can easily go down the hallway to the living room and ask my mom, but I feel like that will make her *too* excited. When I first let it casually slip that I was going to a boy's house for family dinner, I was worried she would have a stroke. This was better than she'd ever hoped for, especially this year. I told her we were just friends, but deep down, I wonder if that's all this really is.

Whenever I think of River, Callista starts to creep back into my mind. I'm grateful in a way—I was so focused on my fear of forgetting her that I wasn't living in the present. Meeting River this summer has shown me that I can start to feel again—hope again—and she will still be there, sprinkled into the little things in my life. Sprinkled into moments like these when I wonder what she would do, what she would wear, why she couldn't be here for me in this moment. Callista is the other half of me that I haven't seen in so long. The half of me that steps out of my comfort zone, talks to new people, goes to family dinner with the boy they just met.

I dig through the now half-empty drawers, empty as a result of my growing pile of shirts on the floor, and decide on a cream top. Plain, family-friendly, and girl next door. The safest option, and it screams Avery Hill. If Callista were here, she would force me to wear the maroon top sitting in the back of my closet, even add a touch of lipstick. But tonight, I want to feel like myself, down to the bone.

Once I slip out of the apartment's front door after an excruciating high-five from my mom, a blast of humid air hits me in the face. I start to walk slowly to the address River gave me that night at the bonfire. I know his neighborhood well, as I do every neighborhood in Destin, and there is no need to rush. Looking at my phone screen, I am thirty minutes early, and it is only a ten-minute walk. This often happens when I overthink, like I tend to do. It used to work out perfectly when it was Callista and me—her tendency to always be fashionably late and mine to be annoyingly early had clashed and resulted in us always being on time.

The sun has almost set by the time I turn the corner onto Sungrove Terrace, yet I am still ten minutes early. River's front lawn is the only one in the neighborhood that isn't covered in grass and blooming flowers of vibrant colors—instead, it is filled with small stones and pebbles and scattered tiny succulents and large cacti. I'm about to step up to the door and debate whether to knock or ring the doorbell when it swings open with a creak. I jump back with my hand to my heart, and River's laugh echoes down the driveway. I'm almost jealous when I see how effortlessly perfect he looks in a plain blue T-shirt and white shorts. He would never spend an hour in his closet, rifling through shirts and wondering what would make him look most presentable.

"I was waiting for you to ring the doorbell, but you stood there gawking for so long I started to wonder if you were ever going to."

"Shut up," I say, my face turning a bright crimson.

"That's no way to speak to your dinner host, is it?" he teases as he leads me inside.

His house is exactly the way I'd imagined it to be—warm-toned with wooden floors, with walls and shelves covered with photos of River and a younger boy I assume to be his brother. I try to ignore the way my knees are starting to weaken at the thought of eating with his entire family.

"You were watching me," I say, trying to hide how nervous I am.

"What?"

"You wouldn't have known I was gawking for so long if you hadn't been watching me," I say triumphantly.

It is now River's face that flushes, and he gives me a sheepish grin as he leads me into the kitchen. It is a charming and narrow space, blue tiles reflecting the last of the setting sun. A brown-haired woman in an apron stands over a pot as the younger boy from the photos stands on his tiptoes to see. Upon hearing our arrival, the woman spins around and smiles at me so big that I can't help but smile back.

"You must be Avery," she exclaims, swooping me into a hug.

I am surprised at how welcoming she is, but I appreciate the ice being broken immediately. River's younger brother stands at a distance, picking his nose shamelessly.

"You're pretty," he says.

"Thank you," I laugh, while River gives him an exasperated look.

"This is Josh," River says. "Ten years old and the household menace."

"I am not," Josh yells as he skids in his socks out of the kitchen.

River's mom is shockingly warm, asking me questions and nodding intently for the rest of the time she prepares food

73

on the stove. When it comes time to set the table, the sky is a dark-tinged purple, light fading into the roaring ocean that sounds through the windows. A man in a navy suit sits at the head of the table, and I recognize him as River's dad from the family portrait on the wall. He smiles at me, just as warmly as River's mom did, and I'm surprised by how comfortable I feel around River's family. I can't recall the last time I had Italian food, and Risotto has never smelled so good.

Family dinner is less formal than I expected it to be, despite River's dad wearing a full suit and tie. Josh is constantly flinging his spoon around, and his parents are continuously smiling at me every other minute. I can tell what River meant by needing to "prove he had friends." How many people does he bring home? I realize that I'm honestly not one to judge, knowing that my mom would have had a similar, if not more extreme, reaction had I brought someone to dinner.

It is almost 8 o'clock when I finish the last of my cookie-crumble ice cream—courtesy of Josh—and River meets my eyes from across the table. He collects everyone's plates, and I follow him into the kitchen as the chattering continues from the dining room.

"So, how was dinner?" he questions with a smile.

"Your family is pretty amazing," I say, almost wistfully.

He looks at me as he puts the dishes in the sink.

"Do you have any siblings?" he asks.

I shake my head. "Only child."

"Ah," he says jokingly. "That explains a lot."

"What is that supposed to mean? I'm just getting used to the feeling, anyways." I shove him gently.

He tilts his head, and I explain further.

"Callista was practically my sister." I want to say more, but it doesn't feel right.

River steps back and looks at the ticking clock above the stove.

"I have an idea."

"An idea?" I'm taken aback.

"It's only eight-thirty, and the night is still young."

I scoff at him. "The night is still young?"

He rolls his eyes at me. "Just go with it. I want to show you something."

I raise my eyebrows at him.

River turns out to be more convincing than I thought he was, and it is pitch black outside. Despite the occasional gust of ocean wind, the night is humid and warm. My top sticks to my back from sweat, and my hair is plastered to my forehead. I shake it off and glance at River.

"Where are we going?" I ask.

"You'll see," he says seriously.

We pass by the boardwalk, and I watch as the flickering lights of the Ferris wheel change color to color. As we make our way further down, something in my stomach drops.

"You're taking me to the dock," I accuse. I stop walking.

He slows down, too, and turns to look at me.

"I am," he says.

"Why?" I almost whisper, blinking fast. I haven't been to the dock since the day of Callista's accident, and I haven't planned on going back. There has never been any reason for me to go to the dock, anyways. Callista was the one who would go out on yachts every weekend, speed boating with the guys from school.

"You haven't been there since it happened, have you?" River asks, knowing the answer.

I swallow. "What does that have to do with anything?"

"You said you were still getting used to it. This will help."

He continues walking, and for some reason, I catch up with him.

"I'm not going on any boat, you know," I say shakily.

He smiles at me. "You don't have to."

When we reach the dock, it looks just like I remembered it that night. Minus the pelting rain, roaring waters, and Callista's eyes flashing at me from the darkness. Ships are lined up in a row—yachts, speedboats, and a singular rowboat off to the side. The street lights flicker up above, temporarily giving way to the darkness of the night sky. Through the haze, clouds start to drift up above, billowing and gray. They look almost cartoon-like, large and moon-lit. I close my eyes, and it feels just as if it is one year ago. Instead of River standing at my side, there's Callista, smirking as she unties her dad's boat.

I feel a drop of water hit my forehead and open my eyes suddenly, shaken back into reality. River is smiling at me, standing quietly and watching my reactions.

"Was that a raindrop?" I say, breaking the silence.

His forehead creases. "It's not raining."

I wipe my forehead only to find it seemingly dry. Nature can be quite cruel sometimes, and it is like the sky is testing my strength. River starts to untie the tiny wooden rowboat from its post, and my mouth drops open.

"You said we weren't going out," I accuse him.

He looks at me. "It's up to you; if you change your mind. But it is a perfect night."

He's right, and the waters look clear and calm, the constant *shhhh* of the waves calming my intrusive thoughts.

I swallow uneasily. I never really thought about another

time I would be out on the sea. I didn't swim or sail, so it never really came to me to worry about it. I guess I subconsciously assumed that I would never go into the ocean again after the accident happened. River can see the doubt on my face, and he starts to re-tie the rowboat.

"It's okay, Avery. We can go back. You're already here; that takes a lot," he says gently.

Something about his tone reminds me of Callista's that night, but unlike her, I know he means what he is saying. If I don't say anything, he will continue to tie the boat and we will leave, accomplished. *I'm already this far.*

"Wait," I say, my voice thick.

He stops.

"I want to," I say.

He nods knowingly and starts to untie the boat again. I stand back and watch him, hands working the knot. The street light makes his hair look more auburn than brown, and when he turns around to smile at me, I realize something. Throughout my entire life, I've never felt so comfortable around someone. Even with Callista, it was always being pushed outside of my limits or shoving my feelings down. With River, I am perfectly calm. I am content.

"We won't go far," he promises me as he takes my hand and leads me into the small boat.

The momentary touch sends electric tingles down my spine, and I shiver.

"Is this really a good idea?" I say, my knees starting to buckle as I realize what I'm doing.

He sits down across from me and grabs an oar.

"The boat is safe. She's small but mighty," he says as he starts to row.

My stomach lurches as I feel the waves slosh up against the side of the boat, and I shut my eyes tightly.

"Are you okay?" River asks gently.

I nod, not opening my eyes. He rows in silence, and I can feel how slowly the boat is going despite the lapping waves around us. I have forgotten this feeling—the one of adrenaline and excitement and worry. I lay down, face up, and open my eyes. River has stopped rowing, and I can feel the movement of the ocean under my back.

We drift peacefully, and I look up at the stars littering the sky above. It's been so long since I've seen a sight like this— the night sky above the ocean, stretching on forever and ever. The stars shine so brightly, and for a moment, I see Callista's face up in the constellations. Her eyes twinkle at me in that playful way they always did, full of promise.

A raindrop falls from the sky and onto my cheek, and my heart drops into my stomach. I realize I was right about the rain before, and memories of the rainwater and saltwater coming together to block the air from reaching my lungs come flooding back.

"River," I start to gasp, but he has already started to turn the boat around.

"I'm so sorry," he breathes, realizing the rain has taken me back.

I put my hand on his arm to stop him, and he does.

"Let's just stay here for a while," I whisper.

He nods in silence, and the rain starts to pour down harder. I lean my head back to catch the rain on my cheeks, streaking down my face, and I have never felt so free. Through my blurry vision, the tiny constellations glitter up above, and once again, Callista is smiling down at me. Something that isn't rainwater trickles down my cheek, and my eyes burn. I can't stop, and all of a sudden, I am laughing and crying all at once, for the first time, and my chest is burning, but it feels so good, and I don't ever want this feeling to go away.

"Avery …" River starts to say, and he reaches over, wiping a tear off my cheek with his thumb.

I am holding on to every feeling, and at this moment, all I can feel is the thundering of my heart and the butterflies that litter my stomach. I close my eyes as the rain comes down harder, faster, and suddenly we are kissing, what's left of my strawberry ChapStick mixing with the salty water on his lips. This is what a first kiss should be like, not in a party basement in the seventh grade with someone who didn't know your name fifteen minutes before—forced by your best friend and an empty soda bottle.

I leave everything behind.

When we pull apart, and I look into his eyes, I realize that they are not the same color as mine. This color is richer, deeper, so deep I can feel honey melt down my throat and coat my tongue with its gritty sweetness.

CHAPTER FOURTEEN

RIVER

This is what summer should be like. Happy, free, not a care in the world. I do have plenty of things to worry about, but summer is to take time off. I don't have to think about anything for at least another month. This past week has made my summer the best one so far, which is saying a lot. I'm almost not sure if it's because our annual family trip to Maui has been canceled this year—a week-long getaway in which I'm stuck babysitting an extra-hyper Josh, sporting matching Hawaiian shirts—or because of Avery Hill.

Avery is like nobody I've ever met before, which sounds cheesy but is true. Everyone at school—or in Destin, for that matter—views me as quiet, disconnected, rude even. It's not because I'm shy or uninterested; it's because none of them would even take the chance to get to know the real me. Avery somehow sees right through me. I'm not sure if she even realizes it.

I remember the first time I saw Avery Hill, laughing away in homeroom. It was freshman year, and she had been attached to Callista Kobb's hip like one of the charms on those designer belts the girls in her group wore every day. No matter how hard she laughed or how wide she smiled, it was obvious to me that she was no Callista. Callista shined like the sun, baiting in everyone around her, but Avery was more like the moon. Lit up when Callista was behind her, yet somehow ethereal in a mysterious way when she was on her own. Avery had been doodling that day, as she did every day in homeroom for the entire year. It was always unclear what she was drawing, but I was usually too buried in work to really pay attention. It was when the bell rang and she got up with the rest of the girls to leave that she tossed the crumpled paper into the trashcan and missed. It was pathetic at the time, and I don't know why I did it, but something in me itched to see what she had been focusing on so hard for that half hour. Always scribbling over her desk, hair falling into her face, only looking up when one of the girls would whisper something to her and she would throw her head back and laugh. I had picked up the paper from the ground, smoothing it out as I walked out of the classroom. It was a drawing of a wooden canoe, sleek and small, its shadow a larger sailboat. Although scribbled messily, it somehow added to the detail. I had pocketed it and kept it for years.

The kiss that night after dinner was not something I had ever expected. But I also can't say I expected to consider myself even acquaintances with Callista Kobb's once best friend. Avery and I had something—something I hadn't thought was possible once upon a time. And I didn't want anything to ruin it.

The bell for lunch rings suddenly, and I grab my textbook from the floor under my desk. Making a beeline for the large oak tree, I watch as a few groups of students trickle out of classrooms. Chattering hand in hand, arm in arm, the student body of Henderson High looks happy—or as happy as they can be, considering they are at school in the middle of summer break. My smile matches theirs as I see Avery walking toward me. She is in jeans and sandals today, a green crocheted top hidden behind her long brown hair. Her tote bag nearly hits me as she tosses it on the table in front of me.

"Easy there," I grin.

She laughs and starts to get comfortable on the bench.

"How was your day?" she asks, brushing my shoulder with hers. There is an electric tingle in the air for a second, and I bask in the feeling.

"As good as summer school can get. How was yours?"

She grimaces. "Calculus."

"You have art after," I offer, as if it will make up for hours of math.

"True," she smiles.

"Have you started on your portfolio piece yet?" I ask casually. I don't want to push her, and I know it's something that has been stressing her.

"Not yet ... but I do have an idea," she says mysteriously.

"What's your idea?"

"It's a secret," she teases childishly.

I open my mouth in mock offense.

"Keeping secrets from me?" I joke.

She shrugs. "It's a good one. It'll be worth it."

"It better be."

Avery's attention seems to snap to something else, and I look up. It's Andres, pacing around a table two spots away from us. If he's trying to work up the courage to come talk to me, he's not hiding it very well. Andres glances up while I'm observing him, puzzled, and we momentarily make eye contact.

He looks worse than I've ever seen him before, with dark circles under his eyes, fidgeting with his hands behind his back. Come to think of it, Andres doesn't even have summer classes. He quit the swim team as well, so what is he doing here at school?

Beside me, Avery stands up. I quickly turn my attention back to her and try to shake all my worries about Andres off. She raises her eyebrows at me and half smiles.

"It looks like you guys should ... talk?" she asks.

I shake my head hurriedly.

"No, really, it's okay," I say, partially because I don't want her to leave and partially because I don't want to deal with Andres right now.

But Andres is heading closer to our table, his eyes now set on me. I sigh, looking up at Avery.

"I'll walk you home after school?" I say as she starts to turn.

She nods agreeably, and I watch as she walks away, past Andres and into the school building. Andres sits down on the other side of the table.

"Hey."

I clear my throat awkwardly. "Hey."

Up close, Andres looks a lot worse than what I first saw. His eyes are bloodshot like he's been crying, and his hair looks like he hasn't washed it in days. I furrow my eyebrows.

"Andres, is everything okay?"

He swallows dryly and shakes his head. It looks like he's about to cry, and I realize that out of all the years I've known him, he's never even come close to crying with me. Growing up an athlete with absent parents makes you strong. It hardens you when you're weighed at the gym every morning and pushed beyond your limits to see how long you can hold your breath underwater. I've watched it harden him. So, for something to crack him like this worries me. Scares me. Whatever has happened to Andres is serious. He looks up at me and takes a deep breath; the air seeming to turn cold around us.

"I killed Callista Kobb."

CHAPTER FIFTEEN

ANDRES

It's been a week since I've been to work—or anywhere out of my house—besides the one time I went to Henderson to see River. I almost didn't do it when I saw Avery Hill sitting right next to him at that lunch table Callista used to text me from. But I knew I had to when I saw the way he looked at me, like I was a lost cause. I am, and I know there's no coming back from it. But River deserved the truth, even if he didn't want it. So, I told him everything there was. Everything from the start to last weekend when Akemi fooled me into thinking she actually liked me—only to get information about Callista. River had been surprisingly calm, sitting with me at that table for the rest of the school day. He eventually left to go walk Avery home, which felt wrong to me after telling him everything that went down. I wonder if it felt wrong to him too, and judging by the clouded defeat that flashed in his eyes when he went to meet her, it did.

Akemi's reaction had been the opposite of River's, although I know she tried to play it off. When she first excused herself to use the bathroom, I knew she would never see me the same again. I don't know what I was thinking, to hope that she might. To say I don't know why I ever trusted her in the first place would be a lie. I liked her. A lot. Our time working together at The Cheery Cherry led me to feel like myself for the first time in a year. Her ambition for journalism and writing, always carrying that pink notepad and pen with her everywhere, made me admire her. I admired her up to the point when it hurt me. I still admire her even now. To pretend for that long, to risk and do so much just for a story. That's the type of dedication that is deadly. The type I once had for swimming.

I wonder if she's tried to text or call, but I don't bother to check. Either way, I don't think I could bear it. I am ashamed, more than I have ever been in my life. Now that the word's out, I can feel my future slowly starting to crumble in front of my eyes. It's only a matter of time before Akemi puts the story out and the entirety of Destin—or the world—will see my true colors. Colors I'm not proud of. But I've accepted it as much as I could, and this is what some would call Karma. I deserve this.

My phone has stayed on do-not-disturb mode for the past week, perfect for hiding in my room all day without having to worry about the swim updates I'm somehow still receiving and party invitations from my ex-teammates. I wonder what my parents would do if they were here, but thankfully that's something I likely will never have to worry about.

A knock on the door makes me flinch, and I slowly throw my sheets off. Making my way out of bed, I kick an empty pizza box across the floor. It's probably River, who has been catering to me during my hibernation period. He comes by every day with pizza and a 7-Up, my comfort meal—also what I used to eat at every swim meet between rounds. We sit on my bed and talk for an hour or so—or sit in silence—but it never fails to make me feel a little better, day by day. I don't deserve a friend like him.

When I finally make my way to the front door, I am blinded by the daylight that I haven't seen in so long in my shuttered, dark and damp room. But I don't need to have a clear vision to realize that the people at my door are not River. A series of hollering and whooping sounds, and I see Alex Kernman and the rest of the swim team boys gathered on my doorstep. The cheering dies down in an instant, probably because they've gotten a good sight of me. I haven't showered in so many days that I've stopped counting, and all I can do is eat, sleep, and cry due to my non-stop watering eyes.

"Oh my god, man, what happened to you?" Colin, a first-year, asks incredulously.

I put my hands over my face.

"Guys, you need to leave," I groan, ready to shut the door.

Alex puts his hand on the door to stop me from shutting it.

"Are you serious, dude?" he shakes his head.

I'm in no mood to deal with everyone, especially the people I've been avoiding for around a month.

"Guys, just ... leave me alone," I sigh, defeated.

A few of the guys step back off the doorstep, muttering to each other or shaking their heads. Alex doesn't back down.

"You know, you've changed since last year," he starts.

"Shocker. People change," I snap as I push against him to close the door.

"We really hoped you'd be back to normal by now," Alex says nastily. "But you know what? I know a lost case when I see one. You remember Jack Chalet, team captain before you? How he was too weak to handle it all, so he just crumbled? You're just like him. Too far gone."

I bite my tongue so hard I taste blood. Before I can slam the door, Colin steps up again.

"Coach wanted us to give this to you."

He tosses the envelope at my feet, and it's addressed from the University of Florida. My stomach lurches. The door slams.

CHAPTER SIXTEEN

AKEMI

The glow of my computer screen lights up my dark room as rain patters on my rooftop. The alarm clock on my nightstand reads 1:45 AM, but I promised myself I wouldn't sleep until I have something typed out on this blank document. A sentence, an idea, anything. I'm desperate. I would have thought that getting my story—especially one so riveting, unexpected, and quite literally life-changing—would have propelled me to the end of at least one page by now. But for some reason, I can't write. That reason being none other than Andres McQueen.

After what happened at the Beachside Bistro, he hasn't shown up to work. I didn't expect him to at first, but now that a week has passed, I'm beginning to wonder if he's ever coming back at all. Every time I walk into The Cheery Cherry, my stomach fills with dread that doesn't leave until the last minute of my shift. Dread that either Andres might come back and I might actually have to face him, and also dread that I have to endure yet another long shift without my coworker, who I had grown so fond of over the past few weeks.

Seeing the look on his face at the restaurant after he found my notebook has left me scarred. It is as if he had turned my hands to stone with that betrayed look, and now I can't type, can't write, can't even take notes. I look over at the clock.

2:00 AM.

I shut the laptop screen and feel an immense pit of guilt

in my stomach as the light slowly dies. *Will I ever be able to write this article at all?* My future as a journalist depends on it, something I keep telling myself day and night and every time I look in the mirror. *But what about Andres?* The arrogant jock that had proven to be nothing but a sweet, lost boy after my first shift with him. The boy that had found himself caught in an accident so tragic it had uprooted his whole life. The boy that had dared Callista Kobb to take her best friend into the storm, unintentionally causing Callista's death. The boy that had trusted me with his story and told me as I looked into his eyes so full of desperation and loss.

I grab my pillow and scream into it.

And what about the heart he had drawn on the bill at the restaurant? Purple, my favorite color. I knew how he feels about me, and I used it to play my game.

But what if I had played myself?

What if I feel the same way toward him?

Too many questions, no answers I can think of. But it still doesn't change the fact that Andres has done something unspeakable, accident or not.

I open my laptop and close it again.

CHAPTER SEVENTEEN

AVERY

I sit crisscrossed on the floor of my bedroom, a messily-taped cardboard box in front of me. I did this last year when I couldn't handle anything. It had taken me days to clear my room of Callista. Everything she had owned that held some sort of sentimental value to me is in that box. The box had been shoved in the back of my closet for months, collecting dust, while I tried to forget its existence. I never thought I would be opening it, except for maybe in twenty years to show my kids. But this past week has been life-changing, and I think I'm finally ready. After I was finally able to cry for the first time in a year, something in me has shifted.

I *want* to do this.

I take a pair of scissors and slit the tape holding the box together.

The first thing I pull out is a pair of Prada sunglasses, and a smile spreads over my face. These are the glasses Callista used to wear out every day of the summer. I have a matching pair, courtesy of her, that is also somewhere in the box. We used to walk around the boardwalk sporting our designer glasses and speaking loudly in posh accents. Callista's genius idea, and it had earned us free ice cream, the fear of the local boys, and the respect of store owners who tried to lure us inside their boutiques. One of my better memories with her.

Something purple and fluffy catches my eye, and I dig

through the box to find it. It's Minnie, the stuffed rhino Callista had won for me at the annual boardwalk fair when we were twelve because I was too short at the time to actually be good at darts. I spend the next half hour rummaging through—pulling out jewelry we had made together, the lip-plumping gloss she used to use because she was too young to get lip filler, even the fake I.D. Callista always had on hand. My floor is messy with random stuffed animals, notes, and articles of clothing, but I don't mind. Something catches my eye, and I pull it out, my hand scraping the side of the cardboard box along the way.

Ouch.

It's an empty glass bottle—root beer, the one from middle school. It had been the summer going into our seventh-grade year, and Callista was convinced that we weren't prepared if we hadn't had our first kisses yet. Callista didn't need to worry about anything; she'd had hers in the fifth grade and wouldn't ever stop talking about it. I had told her I wanted my first kiss to be special, something to remember, and it didn't matter if it was in seventh grade or not. But in typical Callista fashion, she had dragged me to Kyle Park's "epic" party, which was really just a damp basement lit with old Christmas lights, a few bean bags tossed on the floor. It was her genius idea to play spin-the-bottle, to none of our surprise, and she had chosen me to go first. I couldn't say no with everyone watching, so I reluctantly spun the old soda bottle, praying for it to at least land on Luka Silva, the cutest guy in our grade. It had landed on Kyle Park himself, who hadn't even known my name when he first let me in the door. The kiss was a quick peck, cold and awkward, but it had been enough for me to stop speaking to Callista for a day. That had been our first fight, also the first time I had stood up for myself.

Something buzzes, and I get up to see if it's my phone. It isn't, and the buzzing sound comes again. I must be crazy, but I swear it's coming from the box. I lean over and brush my hair out of my face as I dig through feather boas and shirts, finally reaching her phone. It can't be—although technically, it could. I had realized after a few months that Callista's parents were still paying her phone bill—she even still had money in her school lunch account. After they moved to California, a long way from Florida and somewhere no storm like that one would hit, it seemed as if they couldn't let go of their daughter. But although her phone was still in service, nobody had tried to contact her in a year. Why now? Is it spam mail? I tap the screen with my shaking index finger and watch as an old picture of Callista and me in the pool lights up. It's a text from ...

Andres?

What?

Andres knows Callista is gone, so why would he be texting her? The last I checked, Callista and Andres weren't close at all. I had seen her occasionally give him flirtatious looks around school, but Callista used to do that with every other athlete on our school's teams. My heart is racing for some reason, and a feeling of dread is creeping up my spine. I enter her passcode with clammy hands—0423—her lucky number combined with her birthday digits.

I wish I could tell you how sorry I am.

My eyes narrow. Then,

I'm so sorry, Cal.

I quickly tap on the text message from him and start to scroll up through their chats, mind racing with a million thoughts. They seem to have talked a lot—and why does his contact name have a heart after it? I freeze when I see my name pop up and let the screen relax.

Got a dare for me tonight?
You're gonna regret asking that ...

Alright, hit me
I dare you to go out in the storm ...

Easy

... but get that Avery girl to go with you

That's it?

At least 2 miles from the coast on boat, and I need pic evidence ;)

She would do anything with me. I'm going to get this point

That prissy girl? Good luck, Cal, but I think you owe me a Yamasaki ;)

You'll see after tonight

My legs seem to give out beneath me, and I fall to my knees, not blinking. That's why she wanted to go out? Not because she had just come up with some stupid idea, but because she was betting on a Yamasaki Jet Ski—the one she had never stopped talking about—on me? And she had actually succeeded in getting me to go out there with her. What if it hadn't been her? What if it had been me? Suddenly, it hits me.

It was never my fault. It was hers. It was Andres.

A hysterical laugh erupts from my throat, and I clap my hands over my face. I start to scroll through the texts again, not even stopping to actually read them. Flashes of words like dare, done, and a series of winky emojis run through my head, and I drop the phone onto my bed, its rhinestone keychain falling to the floor. This is why my life has been completely uprooted. Because of a dare? From Andres McQueen? Captain of the swim team and mega asshole, the one who has been treating me weirdly all summer? Is this why? And Callista, she hadn't told me anything. About the dares, Andres, nothing. And she had let Andres use me, her best friend—I cup my hands over my mouth. I feel like I'm going to throw up. It could have been me who died that day. At this moment, I almost wish it were.

A knock makes me jump, and I feel even more sick. The door swings open, and it's River, leaning against the doorframe carrying a bag of what I assume to be snacks.

"Your mom let me in," he grins.

I can barely see him out of my blurry vision, tears threatening to spill out. He jumps back in alarm when he sees me. "Avery?"

His eyes dart from my face to the phone on my bed to the box on the ground, and when he sees the rhinestone phone case, he starts to connect the dots. He drops the bag on the ground and steps forward. I look at him.

"She—she—"

I can't get the words out. I don't know how to begin, what

to say, if I should say anything at all. But the way he looks at me at that moment, so sad, so pitiful, makes my blood run cold. My breath hitches in my throat as I come to a realization.

"You knew," I say, my voice sounding high and unrecognizable.

He swallows, but doesn't deny it. He takes another step forward. I take one backward.

"You knew?" I ask, voice rising.

He is speechless.

"I'm so sorry, Avery," is all he can say as he looks at me with a sorrowful expression.

I scoff and immediately cover my mouth again, feeling like this time I'm actually going to be sick.

He runs over to hold me up, and I shove him off.

"He's my best friend ..." he says, stepping back.

"*She* was my best friend!" I snap, unbelieving.

His mouth falls open, but I continue.

"You knew, and you let me actually get close to you; you let me *kiss* you?" I shriek.

"I didn't know then—" he starts, but I cut him off.

"Get out."

He closes his mouth in defeat but stands there unmoving. I grab a hand-knit pillow from my bed and throw it at him.

"Get out!"

He does.

Once he's gone, the tears start to flow freely, running down my face and onto the bed beneath me. I make my way to my desk, almost tripping in the process, and pull out my already-sketched canvas and ready-to-go paints. I scribble my sketch out angrily. Through the tears, my vision turns red hot. I grab my canvas and start to paint.

CHAPTER EIGHTEEN

RIVER

I have never been good at resolving issues. With Andres, it's easy because we never fight about the serious stuff. Minus the secret he had kept from me that had flipped my entire summer around and ruined my relationship with Avery. It used to be easy. We would fight about the dumbest things—who got to be which monster truck when we were playing in my bedroom in the first grade, why he got me out in dodgeball, who was faster at the mile. A quick and simple *sorry* had always fixed it, sometimes with an awkward shoulder pat-hug if it was really bad. But I don't know how to fix the real things.

The one time Josh got into really big trouble with my dad was when he shredded half of Dad's important work documents because he wanted to see how the electric shredder worked. I couldn't bear to see the devastated look on Josh's face, so I took the blame for it. I had never apologized for myself. It was always for someone else. But after what I did to Avery, I know I need to make it right. I just don't know how. Now that she knows, it feels like a weight has been lifted off of my chest and a larger one has been placed there. I was so caught up in my guilt that I could barely look at her without shoving it down, but now it's even worse.

I need to see Andres and tell him that she knows. If I can't make it right, he somehow has to. For both of their sakes.

When I arrive at The Cheery Cherry, it is mid-afternoon,

and the sun burns through the back of my T-shirt. Through the glass, I only see Akemi, but Andres has promised he would go back to work. After a week of him shutting himself in his room, only getting up to let me in with his daily pizza delivery, I told him it was time to get himself together. Face Akemi, go back to work before he loses his job, and take a damn shower. But Andres is not behind the counter, and I don't know where else he would be.

"Hey, Akemi," I say as the automatic bell sounds.

She glances up from her notebook.

"Oh, hey, River," she says. She looks exhausted, and I know why.

"Is Andres here?" I ask, and she shuts her notebook.

"He hasn't been in for a while," she replies. She glances down at her shoes behind the counter, and I wonder if she's feeling just as bad as I am. I feel sad for her. She looks up.

"Why? Did something happen?"

I shrug her off. "No, everything's fine. Just haven't seen him in a while ... that's all."

I wave goodbye to her as I leave the shop, angry at Andres and myself.

My next stop is Andres' house, and I know the way all too well. I knock on the door and wait for him to open up, but he doesn't answer this time. Feeling impatient, I unlock it with the spare keys he stupidly keeps under his doormat and step inside.

"Andres?" I call out, waiting for a response.

There is none. I go up to his room, and the door is wide open. Andres is sitting on his bed, staring down at an envelope in his hand. He doesn't look up when I enter his room. I sigh.

"What's that?"

"It's from the University of Florida," he says slowly.

96

"The University of Florida? Have you opened it?" I say as I sit down next to him.

He nods. "They're offering me a scholarship."

My mouth drops open. "You—wow ..." I say, looking down at my hands.

"Even after you quit the swim team?"

"I guess Coach talked to them or something," he mumbles. I'm confused by his tone.

"Isn't this a good thing?" I ask.

He shrugs. It's clear that he doesn't want to talk about it right now, and sometimes Andres needs to work things out on his own.

"I came here to talk to you about what you told me," I say, changing the subject.

He looks up. "Yeah?"

"Avery knows."

He doesn't look surprised, but drops the envelope onto the bed.

"You told her?" he asks.

"No," I say. "She saw your texts on Callista's phone."

He sighs and puts his head in his palms.

I look at him.

"You need to make this right."

He nods, not making eye contact with me, and I know how he feels.

I shake my head and walk out of the room.

The next day at summer school, Avery is still not talking to me. It's been days since she's shown up to the table at the large oak tree, and I feel horrible to think that I've driven her away from her lunch spot. Every day I wait alone at the table to see if she might show up, even for the last five minutes of the break, but she never does. I understand why. I've sent her multiple texts, explaining that I hadn't known before and I didn't know how to tell her, but they all sound like excuses. I don't expect any replies at this point, but I want to find some way to make it up to her.

When I get back home, Josh runs up to greet me.

"Hey, bud," I say, ruffling his hair.

He wrinkles his nose at me. "Your girlfriend is in your room."

I straighten up. "Now? She's in my room now?"

He over-exaggeratingly nods and runs backward into the kitchen.

I make a show of not rushing up the stairs, but my heart is drumming in my chest. Is she here to yell at me? To hear me out?

I open the door, and Avery is sitting on my bed, phone in hand. She is wearing the same white top she wore to dinner that one day, and memories flood back into my mind. I start to open my mouth to say something, anything, but when I see the look on her face, I fall silent. Our eyes meet, and it's like an instant understanding has passed between us. She looks at me quietly and raises her eyebrows.

"Your mom let me in."

CHAPTER NINETEEN

ANDRES

It is a few days later when I finally decide to go back to work. I don't know if I still have a job after my long leave of absence, but the owner is rarely there anyways, and I think I would have gotten a text from Akemi if there was something going on. I mean, I definitely have gotten texts from her—constant apologies and asking if I'm coming to work today—but I haven't felt like answering. When I walk into The Cheery Cherry, Akemi is sitting in a chair at the cash register. She finishes serving a scoop of raspberry sherbet to a little boy in a red cap, then looks at me. She swallows, and it's a strange and new feeling of discomfort that passes through my body when I go to sit next to her.

"Hey," she starts.

"Hey," I reply.

"I'm really sorry about what happened ..." she trails off.

I can see that it really is bothering her, and she tucks a strand of long black hair behind her ear.

I raise my eyebrows. "How's the article going?"

She looks down at her hands. "I haven't written it," she says.

I'm confused. "Why not? You have everything you need, don't you?"

She shakes her head. "It feels wrong after the way you told me."

It's quiet for a moment as I ponder what she means. When she agreed to go out to dinner with me after work, she knew what she was going there for. Why did she change her mind now? I'm also confused about the way she doesn't seem to be treating me any differently. The way she looks at me is still the same, although she knows my deepest, darkest secret and is planning on sharing it with the world.

"Just write the article," I say firmly.

She looks up at me, furrowing her eyebrows.

"You want me to write the article?" she asks incredulously.

I sigh. "Yes."

"Why?"

"Because I deserve it. People should know," I say, feeling kind of sick to my stomach as I admit it.

She shakes her head. "I mean, I agree, but I don't know."

I laugh at how ridiculous this is. "You lead me on for information, and now you're not even going to use it?"

She starts to kind of laugh, too, stopping quickly. "I wasn't trying to lead you on."

I look at her. "Yeah, right. I've been there once."

She glances at me curiously.

I point at my chest. "Swim captain? Sports here aren't so innocent."

She raises her eyebrows. "Maybe I should write an article about *that*."

I turn my whole body to face her, but the bell sounds, and a middle-aged woman walks into the store. I watch Akemi as she scoops dulce de leche ice cream into a cone, hair fluttering into her face. I've really missed this. When the woman has paid and there have been at least two minutes of silence between Akemi and me, I turn to her again.

"I'm going to make this right," I start.

She looks at me. "How?"

"I have a meeting with my coach and someone from the University of Florida after this shift," I say.

Her eyes widen. "The University of Florida?"

I nod. "They sent me a letter. I received that scholarship I wanted so bad."

She swallows. "Wow, that's awesome, Andres."

I shrug. "Maybe."

There's another brief moment of silence before I break it again. "Did you mean it when you said you weren't trying to lead me on?"

She hesitates. "Kind of."

I look at her. "What?"

"I knew how you felt, and I admit that I did use that to my advantage ... but I still liked you too," she mumbles awkwardly.

I'm stunned. "So, it wasn't all fake."

She shakes her head. "Of course not."

We are so close, and for a second, it feels like we might kiss, but Akemi abruptly pulls away and turns to the side. I step back stupidly and clear my throat.

"Not yet," she trails off.

I nod speechlessly.

"I need time," she says quietly.

I look at her. "You're going to write the article?"

She shakes her head. "I don't know."

I give her a sad smile. "Whatever you do, I understand."

It's dark by the time I reach Henderson High School, and I'm so late that I don't bother locking my bike. I jog until I reach the gym, relishing in the feeling of the cool breeze. Coach sits on a bench to the side, a man from the swim meet next to him. I recognize him as one of the recruiters from the University of Florida.

"You're late," Coach says accusingly, and I realize that although I haven't seen him in almost a month, nothing has changed.

"I was at work," I apologize. "It won't happen again."

The man gets up from the bench to shake hands with me.

"It's all good, Mr. McQueen. I'm Calvin Lopez from the University of Florida."

He has a good handshake.

"I know who you are."

Coach stretches his hands in front of him as I sit down.

"The reason we wanted to call this meeting, Andres, is to discuss your dropping of the swim team."

I sigh inwardly.

The recruiter steps in. "The scholarship does require you to continue the swim team throughout your senior year of high school," he says, as if this is new information to me.

I nod. "I know."

Coach looks at me like he's trying to telepathically communicate with me, and I choose to ignore his antics.

"So, are you coming back?"

I shrug. "I'm not sure."

Coach erupts. "Are you crazy? This is your scholarship, boy!"

The recruiter is nodding along with him.

"We've seen your skills, Andres. We really want you. You would make a very valuable addition to our swim team."

Coach looks like he's about to faint behind him.

I look at both of them determinedly.

"I'll do it on one condition."

CHAPTER TWENTY

AKEMI

The burning sand scratches my bare toes as I stretch out on the beach. Avery is next to me, her head on her knees. She texted me last night, asking to meet with me today. It was the first time she'd texted me in years, and I bet she had to dig far back into her contacts to find my number. I have an idea what she wants to talk about, but I'm not sure if she knows Andres' secret.

"Thanks for coming," she says softly.

I give her a genuine smile. "No problem. What's up?"

"I know you wanted an article about Callista, and I'm sorry I wouldn't talk to you before."

I wave it off. "It's fine, really. I'm not sure if I'm going to write that article anyways."

She turns to me. "I have a feeling you're going to want to after what I tell you."

I don't say anything, just look at her solemnly. She opens her mouth in shock.

"No way."

I grimace.

"You knew too?" she asks, covering her face.

"What do you mean 'too'?" I ask.

She tells me about finding out River knew this entire time, and I am shocked. I didn't think Andres would have told River, not after the way they had gotten into that huge fight a few weeks ago.

"So, who told you?" she asks.

I lick my lips. "Andres."

She raises her eyebrows. "Wow. Straight from the source."

I don't say anything.

She continues. "I forgive River because he had nothing to do with it. He really didn't know. Nothing was his fault."

I nod.

"But Andres, he knew exactly what he was doing."

I want to jump in and defend him, but she's right in a way. Even though he hadn't meant for anything to happen, it was still his fault, and he had hidden it from everyone. I let Avery talk.

"I just can't believe Callista would have done that to me. Or—actually, that's a lie. Of course she would have done something like that to me."

I flick sand off my legs.

"You couldn't have known that. You were best friends," I say, almost bitterly.

She shakes her head.

"She wasn't that great of a friend."

I'm shocked at the way Avery is talking about Callista after a year of refusing to so much as utter her name. But I do know what she's talking about, and I lean back.

"Do you remember that one time in eighth grade when we bumped into each other in the bathrooms during class?" she asks.

I nod slowly, the bitter memories coming back to me.

"And Callista took your hall pass because we didn't have one, so you ended up getting in trouble?" she continues.

I nod. How could I forget? It had landed me a week in detention, while Callista had gotten away consequence-free.

"I'm sorry for that," she says.

I cock my head. "That was years ago. It doesn't matter."

She shakes her head. "I'm still sorry."

I look at her.

"You know how you said Andres knew what he was doing?" I ask.

She slowly nods.

"Don't take it out too hard on him," I say.

She glances at me.

"He used me. We didn't know each other. And if he hadn't texted her that ..." she trails off.

"I understand," I say. "But he can't take back what he did. He regrets it; I know him."

She flushes. "I could have been the one that died."

I'm silent. She's right.

"Do you know what Andres is doing right now?" I ask.

She looks at me sideways.

"He's trying to make it right, the best he can," I continue.

She shakes her head. "And how is he going to do that?"

"He was offered a scholarship from the University of Florida," I say.

She scoffs. "He doesn't deserve it."

"He's not taking it," I say.

She slowly looks up.

"Instead, he's using the money to sponsor another scholarship—the Callista Kobb scholarship."

Avery is speechless.

"It's for the Warrington College of Business."

She swallows. "Her dream."

I nod.

Avery looks out at the ocean, waves roaring as the sun sinks into the sea. She doesn't notice when I get up and leave.

When I get home, my parents are sitting on the couch

watching the news like they usually are at this hour. My mom turns to wave at me.

"How is your writing going?" she asks. She knows me too well, and my pink notebook hangs out of my jean pocket.

"It's going good," I say, smiling truly.

When I get up to my room, the first thing I do in so long is open my laptop. I don't bother to flick on the light switch on the wall, but rather let the light of the screen engulf me. I erase the title of the previous document I had been working on and replace it.

Chapter One.

I begin to write the story of two best friends.

EPILOGUE

AVERY

One month Later

River and I sit side by side in one of the bright red booths at The Cheery Cherry. Across from us are our friends Akemi and Andres. There's a moment of peaceful silence as we focus on our ice creams, mine a mint chocolate with extra chocolate chips. Summer is almost over, and I'm grateful. While I've made so many good memories this summer break, there's so much I want to do in the senior school year. Now that I have River, Akemi, and Andres, I know this year will be a good one. Or at least better than last year. I have finished my portfolio piece for the art school I want to apply to, and after photocopying it, I sold it to the nearby art studio as a display piece. It feels right to keep it here, in Destin, overlooking the unpredictable waves of the ocean. I'm glad to say that I have my artistic abilities back, and I spend all Calculus class at summer school doodling in my graphing notebook.

After Callista, I never thought I would find anybody else. But River has shown me that life is full of people you never expected to bond with. River sweeps a piece of hair out of my face while Andres gags from across the table. He tries to do the same to Akemi, but she slaps his hand away. We all laugh.

We're a weird group, when I come to think of it. Akemi and I have always been unlikely friends, with our past and the way Callista came between us. But Andres and I are the unlikeliest friends of all. I can tell why Callista was so close to him—they are alike in so many ways. Andres is spontaneous, constantly up to adrenaline-provoking activities, just like she used to be. He reminds me of her, in a way. Sometimes, I wonder what would have happened if the roles were reversed—Callista daring him to go out into the storm. I think the only reason we are so close now is because of what we've all been through together. Callista's death has impacted all of us—or most of us—in ways we never saw coming and forced us over hurdles we never thought we'd overcome.

The Callista Kobb scholarship Andres had planned is in the works, and I have to say, it is a good start on his long road to recovery.

"What did happen to that article, Akemi?" River asks, breaking the silence.

Akemi and I look at each other. She grins.

"Let's just say it's not an article anymore," she winks.

While River and Andres fight over what that could possibly mean, I stare out of the shop window, spooning melting ice cream into my mouth. For the first time in a while, I can say that I'm genuinely happy.

Momentarily, I make eye contact with my portfolio piece in the art studio window across the boardwalk. The dark blue hues seem to still everything around it, and my chest feels light as I smile.

A girl in the constellations, her familiar eyes twinkling back at me.

ABOUT ATMOSPHERE PRESS

Founded in 2015, Atmosphere Press was built on the principles of Honesty, Transparency, Professionalism, Kindness, and Making Your Book Awesome. As an ethical and author-friendly hybrid press, we stay true to that founding mission today.

If you're a reader, enter our giveaway for a free book here:

SCAN TO ENTER
BOOK GIVEAWAY

If you're a writer, submit your manuscript for consideration here:

SCAN TO SUBMIT
MANUSCRIPT

And always feel free to visit Atmosphere Press and our authors online at atmospherepress.com. See you there soon!

ABOUT THE AUTHOR

KATIA MIYAMOTO is a high school student from Southern California, with a love for both writing and playing the piano. *The Undertow of Healing* is her debut novel, which she started writing during her sophomore year. She is currently working on a second book, and hopes to publish in the near future.

.

Milton Keynes UK
Ingram Content Group UK Ltd.
UKHW010738241123
433194UK00005B/443

9 798891 320819